Praise for Sharon Cullen's *Deception*

Deception - Nominated for a 2009 EPPIE

Deception - Awared the prestigious CataNetwork Reviewers' Choice Award for 2008. Your book, DECEPTION, is one of the best books reviewed on Ecataromance this year

Rating: 5 Nymphs "Deception is a thrill ride you simply must encounter. If action and suspense is what your summer is missing, I suggest you pick up a copy of Sharon Cullen's Deception."

~ *Literary Nymphs*

Rating: 5 Stars "Fans of Tara Janzen's "Steele Street" series will love "Deception" by Sharon Cullen."

~ *Ecataromance*

Rating: 4 Blue Ribbons "The awesome plot was jam-packed with non-stop action, super-hot romance and a thrilling cat-and-mouse game that had my heart pounding with breathtaking excitement."

~ *Romance Junkies*

Rating: 5 Stars   "Deception is a fabulous romantic suspense."

~ *The Long and the Short of It.*

Look for these titles by *Sharon Cullen*

Now Available:

Night Song

Love on the Edge Series
Deception (Book 1)
Redemption (Book 2)
Obsession (Book 3)

Deception

Sharon Cullen

Pattie –
I'm so glad you
enjoyed it. Happy
Reading.
Sharon Cullen

A Samhain Publishing, Ltd. publication.

Samhain Publishing, Ltd.
577 Mulberry Street, Suite 1520
Macon, GA 31201
www.samhainpublishing.com

Deception
Copyright © 2009 by Sharon Cullen
Print ISBN: 978-1-60504-280-0
Digital ISBN: 1-60504-075-4

Editing by Sarah Palmero
Cover by Scott Carpenter

First Samhain Publishing, Ltd. electronic publication: July 2008
First Samhain Publishing, Ltd. print publication: May 2009

Dedication

To Ann Warner, who helped me take this story apart sentence by sentence and build it into the story it is today. And, of course, to John. I love you.

Chapter One

No good ever came from opening a door without looking through the peephole. Or so Kate's mom always said.

Luke Barone leaned against the doorframe, hard, muscular forearms folded over his chest, cool gray eyes staring into hers, proving Mom right.

Kate tightened her already white-knuckled grip on the doorknob. "Go away."

"Kate—"

She slammed the door in his face, spun around and pressed her back against the trembling wood, closing her eyes and willing Luke away. Far away. Back to where he came from. Wherever that was.

"Kate, please, I know you're angry—"

"Angry, Luke? *Angry*? I left angry months ago. I'm not angry anymore."

"Good, because—"

"I'm homicidal."

A small thud shook the door, as if he'd hit it, and Kate jumped.

"Kate?" His voice floated through the solid wood and Kate closed her eyes, picturing him leaning his forehead against the door. "I need you," he whispered.

"No you don't. Go away."

"I do. Please help me."

His voice was like a knife to her heart. No, a knife to her heart would have hurt less. He sounded as if he were in pain. She pushed her compassion away. *Do* not *open that door!* Because opening that door would admit all her demons. Demons she had worked hard to eradicate.

"Kate?"

She had to strain to hear him. As if it had a mind of its own, her hand curled around the doorknob.

"I'm sorry, Kate."

She yanked her hand away. Emotions she had fought so hard to overcome came crashing back. Betrayal, fear. And pain. So much pain.

"You come here *now* to tell me you're sorry? I could have used those words eighteen months ago, Luke. They don't mean anything anymore." She tried to inject a note of anger in her voice but the words came out weary and sad.

A long pause followed and, against her better judgment, she held her breath, waiting to hear what Luke would say next, what excuse he would give, what lie he would tell.

"If you would just let me in," he said, his voice weary. "I'll explain."

She debated, darn her. She debated whether she should let him in. Part of her wanted to. Another part didn't. Both were equally adamant. She stared at the doorknob, trying to decide. *Let him in, not let him in? Listen to his excuses, or give him a piece of my mind?* Then she realized that some time had passed since he'd spoken.

"Luke?"

"Still here." It sounded as if he were speaking through

clenched teeth.

"You okay?" She closed her eyes. Why, oh why, did she care? She shouldn't. Eighteen months of silence from this man told her she shouldn't care. But she did.

"Peachy. Kate, you have to let me in. Please. I don't have anywhere else to go."

She drew back, realizing almost too late that she'd been reaching for the doorknob again. He didn't have anywhere else to go? He came back, *months later*, because he didn't have anywhere else to *go*? "Go back to where you came from," she spit out.

She spun on her heels with every intention of walking away. But a soft sigh drifted through the door and his plaintive voice called to her.

"Kate, don't leave me out here."

Kate's heart clenched as she tried to hang on to her anger. "Don't *leave* you? You mean don't leave you like you left me? Is that what you mean?" Silence. "Luke? Are you listening to me?"

In that first moment, seeing him leaning against her door as if he owned the place, the nightmares had returned. For the past year she'd made strides in her life, had thought she was overcoming that very dark part of her past. Then Luke had shown up and the memories came barreling into her and not only that, her heart had turned over at the sight of him.

He'd looked good. Too good. His dark brown hair was a little longer than she remembered and under that baseball hat, his gray eyes seemed a little sadder, as if he'd seen way too much of the evil side of humanity.

Her gaze went to the door. That wasn't all she'd seen. She'd seen pain, recognizing it because it'd stared back at her in the mirror.

She took a hesitant step toward the door. "Luke? Darn it, did you leave again?" Her counselor's words hung in her mind. *Verbalize your anger, Kate. Don't internalize it.* Well, now would be the perfect time to verbalize. She strode forward. "Oh, no you don't. I've waited a long time to tell you exactly how I feel. No way are you gonna walk out on that, too!"

She yanked the door open. Luke fell backward through the opening and landed in a heap at her feet. Asleep. No, not asleep. Unconscious.

Kate stared down at him in horror. "Oh, Luke, what have you gotten yourself into?"

Luke opened his eyes and rolled off the bed in one swift, painful move. The room spun and he swayed, pressing his knees against the edge of the bed for balance. His gaze roamed the unfamiliar surroundings, cataloguing the layout, searching for escape. His peripheral vision faded and his instincts screamed to get the hell out.

He reached for the gun secured at the small of his back, but the sudden movement made him stumble and he almost fell face-first onto the bed. That's when he spotted Kate on the other side of the room, a phone pressed to her ear.

Fear pushed the pain to the back of his mind. He reached her in two strides and grabbed the phone. "What are you doing?"

Her big blue eyes went wide. "Calling a doctor."

Luke bent down and yanked the phone cord from the wall. "No doctor." The bright colors of the room faded and he swayed, reaching for Kate so he wouldn't fall. She staggered under his weight and grabbed onto his arm, the countless bracelets on her wrist jingling and echoing in his pounding brain.

"Luke, you passed out on my front stoop."

"I passed out on your front stoop because you wouldn't let me pass out inside."

She glared at him. "And you bled all over my bed."

He tried to focus on the blood staining the blue and white comforter, but those annoying black dots danced in front of his eyes. "Sorry," he mumbled. "No doctor."

Kate took his arm and helped him back to bed. "I don't know why you're here or what you've gotten yourself into. Frankly, I don't care. I just want you to leave."

Luke lay back down on the soft comforter and sighed, the room finally righting itself. He looked at Kate, really looked. He'd spent a lot of time remembering her face, her laugh, the twinkle in her eyes. But the Kate before him wasn't the Kate of his memories. The hair that used to curl in blond corkscrews was now merely wavy. Her apple-pie looks had transformed into something...different was the only word that came to mind. And not a good different.

Where she used to wear one pair of earrings, now several pairs glittered in each ear. Dozens of thin bracelets danced along her wrists. She'd always said she didn't like bracelets, claiming they got in the way when she painted.

His gaze traveled those gorgeous legs he remembered so well, noted the cut-off denims that were almost, but not quite, Daisy Dukes. A red tank top stopped a few inches above the cut-offs and—oh, mama! His eyes widened—a silver belly button ring winked at him.

He didn't know if he liked this new person staring at him with her hands on her hips. Hands whose fingers sported several different rings and purple nail polish. She came across as hard and cold. Not the free-spirited woman he'd left.

13

When he'd first met her, that rigid, self-controlled part of him had reached out to her before he could put a rope around it and reel it in. It'd been a mistake. *She'd* been a mistake. A mistake he couldn't seem to regret. After all, memories of Katherine McAuley had pulled him through some horrendous times.

"Well?" She tapped her foot, hands still on her hips, eyes narrowed.

He tried to focus, to remember what it was she had said. Ah, that's right. She wanted him gone. He couldn't blame her, not really. Coming here had not been one of his most brilliant ideas. But then again, he'd been pretty short of brilliant ideas for the past year and a half.

"I'll go as soon as I can. No doctor, Kate. No one can know I'm here."

She stared at him with bright blue eyes rimmed in...*black*. "You left. No note, no call, not even a postcard in the mail saying see you later. I haven't heard a word from you in eighteen months. Now you claim you have nowhere to go? And what the heck happened to you?" Her gaze ran up and down his body and if he weren't feeling like he'd been dragged down the highway by a semi, his body would have responded as it always had when it came to Kate—primitively, wildly. Without thought.

What the heck happened to you? Her words were the catalyst that jump-started his memories. A knife flashing in the light of a streetlamp. Pain. Blood. His home torn apart.

He'd been attacked, beaten, and only by the grace of God left alive. Age-old instincts had told him to go to ground. To run. Hide. Something else told him to go to Kate. Something he wasn't in any condition to think about. He needed to hide out, to heal and most importantly to figure out what was going on. Why he'd been attacked.

Exhaustion lapped at his thoughts and he leaned back against the pillow and closed his eyes, floating on waves of pain. Hovering between consciousness and oblivion, he was all too aware that Kate stood next to him, scowling.

"So what am I supposed to do with you?" she asked.

He managed to grin. She might look different on the outside, but inside she was still his Kate—sassy, brazen and feisty.

"Let me rest. In a few days I'll be out of here." At the thought of walking away from her again, a different sort of pain entered the little fiesta going on inside him.

But leave he must. Especially if his gut feeling was right and this beating wasn't merely a burglary gone bad.

"Days? *Days!*" When he opened his eyes, hers were flashing liquid fire at him. "I don't think so. You have two hours to rest and get out of my life." She pointed to the door, the bracelets sliding up and down her arm, creating a merry tune. "For good this time. I don't want to see you two years or even two hours from now."

Her words injured him more than the knife gash to his side, more than his throbbing ribs. They cut through to his soul. But it wasn't anything he hadn't expected.

"Roll over," she said.

"Excuse me?"

She poked his arm and her bracelets clinked. "Roll over, macho man. You'll be more comfortable under the covers."

He rolled, grimacing at the movement. Underneath her anger—and all that makeup—she seemed concerned and that gave him hope. Not that she'd ever forgive him. Not that he expected her to forgive him.

"You're burning up. You need a doctor."

15

He was fighting for consciousness, the rolling motion causing the room to spin and his stomach to lurch. He couldn't succumb to the enticing appeal of sleep until he convinced Kate not to call a doctor. He grabbed her arm, and the smooth, silky feel of her skin brought memories rushing back. "No doctor. Promise." Sweat popped out on his forehead, his hand shook and his stomach clenched.

She stopped smoothing the bedsheets and stared at him. "What have you gotten yourself into?"

He ignored the question, having no intention of ever telling her. "Promise me."

She sighed. "I promise."

Luke relaxed against the pillow. Kate's promises were as good as gold.

Too bad she thought his weren't.

Kate stared out the window at a warm night bathed in the soft glow of an almost-full moon. Arms wrapped around her middle, she fought the resentment welling inside her as she glanced over her shoulder at the man lying in her bed.

For so many months she'd hoped and prayed Luke would miraculously return to her. Eventually the hope had dwindled to acceptance that he was gone for good. To see him now, well, it was disconcerting to say the least. Troubling would be a better word, but still not close. There were too many emotions she was feeling. Things she'd thought she'd worked through, thought she'd moved away from. But one word from Luke, one look, and her hard-won victories all came crashing down around her.

She didn't want him here. Hadn't been lying when she said she wanted him gone. She didn't have it in her to go back to that point in her life. The place where everything had been perfect, before... Well, just before.

Her mind veered from those dark months when she'd fought for her very sanity. She'd come to realize it hadn't been Luke's fault, yet she still couldn't separate him from the other things that had happened.

She ran a hand through her hair, then dropped it to her side. She'd had to call in sick at work, and since it was a Saturday night, her boss hadn't been too happy. Neither had she, for that matter. Saturday nights brought in a lot of tips and she needed every penny she could lay her hands on just to keep chugging through life. Something she'd been managing pretty well until her past came back to smack her in the face.

I don't have anywhere else to go. Well, wasn't that just great. So he picked her house? Oh, yeah. Luke Barone definitely had to go. But not before he answered some questions.

Behind her, he moaned. It wasn't the first time. Since he'd fallen asleep, or passed out, he'd tossed and turned and mumbled. Kate turned from the window and stared at him, taking in his flushed face. She leaned over and pressed the back of her hand against his forehead, then his cheek. She wasn't a doctor, but even she could tell his fever had escalated. His dry skin burned with it.

Her mother had always given her cool baths when she had a fever, but Kate didn't think she could get Luke to the bathroom, let alone into the tub. He wasn't overly large, but he was muscular and she'd struggled to get him from the front door to the bed. Good thing he'd come to enough to help.

But she needed to get this fever down, to cool him off and to get him out of those clothes. She reached for the buttons on his shirt and hesitated, her hand hovering above his chest. She didn't want to touch him. Not so intimately at least.

He moaned again and she shook herself free of her fear. *It's*

Luke, you ninny, and he's in pain. She *hated* to see anyone suffer—even Luke. With quick fingers, she unbuttoned his shirt and spread it open, revealing a chest she'd hoped she'd forgotten but found she remembered too well.

Most of it at least.

He was covered in bruises, but they weren't what held her attention. At one time she'd known every dip and valley of Luke's body, and those scars hadn't been there before. Some were small, others large, some faded to a silver white while others were pink and puckered. The pictures she'd formed of him lounging on the Riviera vanished, replaced with visions her mind shied from.

Her anger began to melt, forming a small puddle in the pit of her stomach. Whoever had beaten him made sure to keep clear of his face, concentrating instead on his torso. Nasty black-and-blue bruises dotted his chest and stomach, some still a vicious red, while a long gash on his side oozed blood.

He shifted, turning his head to the side. She pulled his arms out of the sleeves and slid the shirt out from beneath him. Next she reached for his fly before pulling back and closing her eyes.

This was torture.

With detached movements a nurse would approve of, Kate unsnapped the jeans and lowered the zipper. Shimmying the denim down his legs took some work, but she managed. Luke grunted a few times and rolled to the side. She froze. Underneath him lay a *gun*. A big, black, lethal-looking thing.

No one can know I'm here.

She stared at Luke, at the cool glow of moonlight touching his skin, highlighting some parts, dipping others into shadows. He was a beautiful man—sleek, powerful. She'd thought, in the year they'd been together, she'd known him pretty well. He'd been funny, kind, generous and oh-so loving.

But never dangerous.

She reached out, and using her thumb and forefinger like she'd seen it done on *Law and Order*, picked up the weapon, set it very carefully on the nightstand, then dusted her hands off.

"Where've you been, Luke? What happened to you?"

She leaned over, examining the scars and the wound. It was red and swollen and looked painful. He moved, shifting his legs and turning his head, mumbling incoherent words. The moon now bathed his flushed face, his cheeks and jaw darkened with a few days' growth of beard. His dark brown hair was mussed. Lighter hair covered his chest, tapering down chiseled abdominal muscles. Kate reached out to those muscles, her cool hand touching hot skin. He muttered again, shifting restlessly.

"No! Pare. No mas, no mas!"

Kate jumped. Luke whipped his head back and forth. His brow creased, his hands clenching the sheets until his knuckles turned white.

She stared at him, dumbfounded. Where had he been for the past eighteen months that he now spoke Spanish?

"Kate!"

She jumped again. He was still out, deep into his dream, or hallucination.

Or memory.

"Kate." He reached out to her, eyes closed. "Help me."

The pleading timbre of his voice touched something deep inside her and melted what little remained of her resistance. Whatever had happened, wherever he'd been, she had a feeling it hadn't been good. *Help me.* Those two words touched her, burned a path right to her heart. She was a sucker for a person in need and apparently, Luke Barone was in desperate need.

She dropped to her knees and grabbed his searching hand, pressing his knuckles to her lips. "I'm here, Luke. You're okay. I'm here."

Chapter Two

Kate ransacked her medicine cabinet, reading labels and tossing aside one bottle after another. "It's here somewhere," she muttered, then cursed herself for not being very organized. Actually, "not very organized" was a gross understatement. She planted her hands on her hips and stared at the now-empty cabinet. Prescription bottles, ibuprofen bottles, tampons, toothpaste, nail polish and various other odds and ends littered the floor. She snapped her fingers, turned on her heel and waded through the mess to get to the kitchen.

"Ah-ha!" She pulled the ampicillin off the shelf, congratulating herself on never throwing anything away. For some reason she could no longer remember, she'd put it with her spices. After grabbing her last clean glass and filling it with water, she hurried back to her bedroom, the precious pills clutched in her hand. Luke was still restless and Kate dropped to her knees beside the bed to touch his cheek.

"Luke?"

"No hablo Español."

She bit back a snort. For the past hour he'd done nothing *but* speak Spanish. "Luke, wake up. You need to take some medicine."

He turned his head away. "No."

She smoothed the hair from his forehead. "Luke, honey, it's

Kate."

The dank, musty scent of the prison cell assaulted him. Only meager cracks of sunlight penetrated the chinks in the thick walls. Night or day, it didn't matter here. His eyes were little use in the dim light. His other senses had taken over.

The wet, spongy odor of mold growing on the stones.

The scurry of the rats as their claws bit into the rough floor.

The laughter of his guards and sometimes the throaty voice of a female.

He didn't know how long he'd been here. Weeks, months, possibly a year. Time meant nothing.

Please, God, let me die.

Lately the beatings had escalated but his body stubbornly refused to give in to his mind's demand. He lived. He breathed. And God help him, he dreamed.

Kate appeared in his dreams, her laughing blue eyes, her cool smile, the warmth of her body. She'd reach out and touch him and he *felt* her. For those precious hours, the Peruvian prison was the dream and Kate the reality.

In his sleep he would hold her, caress her, make love to her on a field of green grass with the stars and the moon looking down on them. He'd kiss her and promise her forever. When he'd awaken, his body curled into a tight ball on the cold, damp floor of his jail cell, he'd know—Kate was the dream, Peru the reality.

He also knew, in those moments between sleep and waking, the reason he didn't die was because he refused to give up those precious hours with Kate in his arms—even if it was only in his mind.

"Luke, honey, it's Kate."

He stilled, then smiled. She'd returned to him tonight. "Kate?"

"Right here."

"Hold me."

"All right."

Soft skin touched his chest. Arms wrapped around his torso. He flinched in pain and her warmth disappeared.

"Don't go."

"I won't." Her voice filled his mind and pushed away the horror. He wanted to talk to her, but exhaustion nibbled at the corners of his mind.

Suddenly the voices of the guards intruded. A low laugh reached his ears and he pushed at Kate's arms. "Get out," he whispered.

"Shhh, it's okay. You're safe."

No. He'd never be safe again. "Go, Kate. Run. Get away before they find you."

"There's no one here, Luke. You're safe, I promise."

The cell door burst open and a guard stood at the entrance, a club clutched in one hand.

Too late. They'd caught him with Kate.

"So you let him go." Suzanne Carmichael leaned back in her executive chair and fiddled with a paper clip, flipping it end over end. The only sound in the long pause that followed her statement was the gentle clack as the clip hit her blotter.

Hank Stuben shifted his bulk from one foot to the other.

She pointed the paper clip at him. "You let him go," she repeated, her tone even, with no hint at the fury inside waiting to be unleashed.

Stuben's eyes went hard, his large, muscular body stilled. "I didn't *let* him go. We would've been caught if I hadn't given the order to leave. Besides, he was in no condition to go anywhere on his own."

"But he did. He got away and now he's gone." The thought still infuriated her. What had started out as an easy solution was quickly getting out of hand and she was spending more time than she liked on this situation.

Stuben's biceps flexed. "The point is, I didn't get caught. Because if I'm caught," he pointed a finger at himself, then at her, "you're caught."

She didn't bother correcting him on that matter. She'd make sure she'd never be caught. But still, the little problem of Luke Barone wasn't to be taken lightly. "Your men were supposed to make it look like he walked into a burglary, yet they didn't take anything." She once again flipped the paper clip. "What happened?"

Stuben shrugged. "They're street thugs. I don't pretend to know how they think."

"Ah, but isn't that what I *pay* you for?"

For the first time since he'd walked into her office, the smug look left his eyes, replaced with something close to fear. Every once in a while she had to rein Hank Stuben in, remind him who was boss. And who was not.

She dismissed him with a wave of her hand. She should punish him somehow for his incompetence but she had a feeling she'd be needing him in the near future. Silently and probably with a great deal of relief, Stuben exited her office and closed the door behind him.

Suzanne stood and turned to the large picture window behind her desk, surveying the most powerful city in the world. Washington D.C.. This could be hers. Very soon it would be hers. Her husband, Bradley, was so close to winning his party's nomination for president of the United States and Suzanne would walk beside him as first lady. Not a bad deal, if she did say so herself. Not bad at all.

She'd worked hard, did what she'd had to, played the game. It was all within reach, right there at the tips of her fingers. Until Luke Barone had discovered her plans. He had to go. She hadn't worked this hard, for this long, to see it all fall apart now.

She fought to contain her anger and the thread of fear snaking through her. The paper clip in her hand bent. If Luke really had heard that conversation as Bradley believed, then everything she'd worked for could be ruined and long-held secrets revealed. And now that he'd been attacked, he'd be even more careful. And mad as hell.

She let loose a string of curse words.

If he didn't want to be found, he wouldn't be. Not even she, with her endless resources, would be able to unearth him. She tapped the paper clip on her bottom lip, looking out the picture window at the cars inching along Dupont Circle.

"Where are you, Barone?"

She'd followed the few leads they had and traced him to Ronald Reagan National Airport, where his trail had gone cold. She wouldn't put it past him to have had a separate identity already laid out for just such an emergency. With it he could have either flown out, in which case he could be anywhere in the world, or rented a car, which meant that after four days he could be almost anywhere in the U.S. Or he could have doubled back and stayed somewhere in the area.

The possibilities were endless. Without knowing his new identity, she didn't have a starting point. However, he was badly hurt, he would need to lay low for a few days. So in all probability he was somewhere near, and if that were the case, she'd find him.

She turned back to her desk and the file the agency kept on all its operatives. She'd been through it a dozen times, discounting one scenario after another. He wouldn't run to his sister, his only surviving family member. It was well known he didn't get along with her. He had few friends, and those leads had already been exhausted. Then something caught her attention, something she'd overlooked before. An Ohio address. She vaguely remembered that Luke had lived somewhere in Ohio a few years ago.

Suzanne put the file down and leaned back, letting her mind wander. Ohio. Flashes of memory came to her. Luke riding in the transport plane, near death, while medics worked on him. He'd been delirious, calling out a name.

Kate.

Ah, now she remembered. For a time, before Peru, Luke had spoken of maybe quitting the organization, settling down. Because of an artist he'd met while on assignment in Cincinnati, Ohio. At the time, Suzanne had chalked it up to burnout, had given him the leave he'd asked for. After Peru, he'd never returned to Ohio, and Suzanne had all but forgotten about it. What was the woman's name? She tapped the bent paper clip on the blotter again.

Kate. Kate. Katherine.

Katherine McAuley.

Certainly Luke wouldn't have run straight to Kate, would he? A few more taps of the paper clip as her mind sorted and catalogued information, things she knew about Luke, what his state of mind would have been as he raced out of D.C. broken and bleeding, confused but still operating as the trained warrior he was.

Yes. Yes, he might. He'd run to Kate thinking she was safe because the only people who knew about her were in the organization. And he would never think the organization would go after him.

Too bad he was wrong.

The purring of the jet engine pulled him from a deep sleep, but he refused to open his eyes, intent on catching a few more Zs before the aircraft landed and he started his next mission.

The rumble of the engines abruptly ceased, and in his half-wakened state, Luke tensed against the expectation of the sudden freefall.

It never came.

He opened his eyes and stared into the slitted eyes of a...cat. He blew out a breath. He'd fully expected to see the inside of a troop transport or a 747. Instead a gray tabby sat on his chest with its front legs curled beneath its body. Confused, Luke shifted, the movement sending shafts of pain racing up his side and tearing a groan from him. The cat uncurled itself and dug its claws into his skin.

Luke winced on a hiss of pain and pushed the cat away. It plopped on the floor.

He touched his aching side and felt the long gash beginning to scab over. He was unprepared for the rush of memories. The fight in Georgetown where he'd been beaten and left for dead in his own home, the desperate need to flee and the agonizing

27

drive to get to Kate. After that it got hazy. He must have passed out, because the next thing he remembered was his prison cell. He ran a hand down his face and pushed those memories away. They haunted him from time to time, not nearly like they had, but often enough.

Gritting his teeth against the pain, he braced his arms and scooted up in the bed. The room tilted and a trickle of sweat rolled down his temple. Ignoring his weakness, he looked the place over, and then remembered the rest. Falling into Kate's house, her anger and eventual help.

If he didn't know her so well, he would have thought she'd been the victim of a burglary. Clothes were thrown in piles—on the floor, on the bureau, a few garments draped over the mirror.

His gaze fell on her, folded into the chair in the corner. Not his version of Kate, but a different one. She wore a flowing muumuu-type thing covered in swirling rainbow colors that hurt his eyes. Her hair lay over one shoulder.

"Hello, Kate."

Her black-rimmed eyes narrowed. The cat, who Luke now remembered was named Picasso, strolled across the room and leapt into Kate's lap where he curled up and fell asleep. Kate stroked Picasso's ears, the light tinkling of her bracelets breaking the tense silence. Never once did her gaze leave his. "How do you feel?"

"Better."

"You ready to talk about why you're here?"

"I told you—"

She waved her hand in the air, effectively cutting him off. "Yeah, yeah, you told me. You didn't have anywhere else to go. So, you going to tell me what happened to send you here or do I have to finish what someone else started and beat it out of you?"

He chuckled but the pain in his ribs stopped him fast. He was surprised, having thought she'd ask the other set of questions: Why'd he leave, where had he been all these years? In a way, those would have been easier to answer.

No, take that back. None of the questions Kate might ask would be easy. Each in their own right was a minefield rife with disaster.

"I deserve to know," she said.

Probably. But that didn't mean he was going to tell her anything. Of course, he had to tell her *something*. He couldn't just suddenly show up on her doorstep, beaten and bloody, without some sort of explanation.

"Just tell me this. Am I in danger by having you here?"

"No." That he could say with certainty. The kind of enemies who would do something like this knew nothing of his connection to Kate McAuley and he planned to keep it that way. "Just give me a few more hours and I'll be out of your hair."

She looked doubtful and he couldn't blame her. He probably looked like something Picasso dragged in, but already he was feeling better. Wiped out, but better.

Kate settled into her chair. "So tell me what happened."

Stick as close to the truth as possible. That was his cardinal rule and had served him well in the past. "I was jumped."

"Where?"

"D.C. Georgetown."

A look of surprise crossed her face. "I'm thinking this wasn't a random mugging or you wouldn't be here."

"No. Not random." He'd realized that right off the bat when the culprits left him with his Rolex and a wallet full of cash, his house trashed, but nothing missing.

"So, what? Enemies?"

"You could say that."

Kate suddenly leaned forward and Luke braced himself for what was to come next. "Tell me, Luke, what type of enemies does an accountant have?"

You wouldn't believe. "Forensic accountant."

She leaned back. "Ah, yes. Forensic accountant."

Forensic accounting had been his cover for years and the career Kate believed he followed. It worked well for his line of work. Forensic accountants worked for law enforcement, both local and federal. They could be called away at a moment's notice and be gone for months at a time. It could be a somewhat dangerous occupation considering forensic accountants could possibly deal with organized crime and the like. It'd been a good cover.

"So you were jumped and beaten and then you left D.C. without calling the cops."

She was like a dog with a bone, and while normally he would admire that trait, right now it annoyed him.

"At least I'm assuming you didn't call the cops."

He probably should have. Not the cops per se, but Suzanne. Suzanne would know what was going on, or at least be able to put some feelers out to determine just how the hell his cover had been blown and who was after him. While he was capable of working blind, he preferred information. Lots of information. Especially if someone was gunning for him.

That thought had him surging out of bed and pushing away the wave of nausea and the blackness closing in.

"What are you doing?"

"Getting dressed. Where are my clothes?"

"You shouldn't be up yet." Alarm crept into her voice.

"Where are my clothes?" he asked again.

He swiveled at the waist and stared at her. "I'm not playing games, Kate. I want my clothes." This suddenly had become much more complex than he'd anticipated. Driving to Kate's house had seemed like a good idea at the time, but then he'd been nearly unconscious. He could barely comprehend how he'd made it all that way without wrecking the car. But now he needed to move on for several reasons, one of which was he didn't want to put Kate in danger. The other being the feelings he still harbored for her. Feelings he'd carefully locked away for years and which now threatened to tear down all his carefully erected shields.

Her wide-eyed gaze bounced over his body, sliding away then coming back, realizing he was about as naked as one could get. "I need my clothes, Kate. I need to get out of here."

"You're in no condition to go anywhere. You had a fever and I had to shove large quantities of antibiotics down your throat."

"I appreciate that, I really do. But I need to go."

"Wait until tomorrow at least."

He wondered what had made her change her mind. Earlier she'd been adamant he leave as soon as possible.

As if sensing his thoughts, she licked her lips and looked away. "If what you say is true, if someone is after you, you're in no shape to deal with them. If you say I'm safe, then stay here until you've recovered."

He glanced out the window at the sun dipping low in the sky. "How long have I been here?"

"Close to twenty-four hours."

He should call Suzanne, but the thought of spending one more night with Kate, of getting a good night's sleep before moving on, appealed to him. If what he guessed about Suzanne

31

was right and there were powerful enemies after him, he had a rough road to haul in the next several days, trying to keep a low profile while discovering what exactly he should do. One more night wouldn't make a difference.

"So tell me about Jay Lang."

Okay, maybe one more night would make a difference. He sighed and ran a hand through his hair. "You went through my wallet."

"Well, yeah." She rolled her eyes. "Who are you?" This last was whispered and the tremor in Kate's voice made his heart do a funny ka-boom.

He settled back in the bed, rearranging the sheets across his legs and lap, trying to figure out what to say, where to start unraveling all the lies. He still couldn't believe they'd been together for nearly a year while he lived a double life. The guilt, at first, had been incredible, but as time had gone by, it got easier and easier. It'd been for her own good. For her protection. He'd had to keep reminding himself of that.

So, who was he? To be honest, he wished he knew. It depended on what day you asked. He could be anything the organization wanted him to be. In fact, it had been his ability to blend in, to become anonymous, that had gained the notice of Suzanne Carmichael. Who was he? No one good, that was for sure. "I'm Lucas Barone."

"So who's Jay Lang?"

"My cover."

A long pause followed in which Luke debated telling Kate everything, regardless of the consequences or the oaths he'd taken to Uncle Sam. The only thing that stopped him was, once again, his concern for her safety. The less she knew the better.

"What have you gotten yourself into?" she asked and he vaguely recalled she'd asked him that before but he'd been in too much pain to answer.

"I don't know. But I plan to find out. That's why I need to get out of here." Already he could feel his energy waning, the exhaustion pulling him under. It took considerable effort to keep his eyes open and it felt like his body weighed a thousand pounds as it pressed into the softness of the bed. Sleep called to him and he was powerless to stop it.

He cursed his weakness even as he succumbed to it.

Chapter Three

A hand clamped down over Kate's mouth. Her eyes flew open, her mind going from slumber to terror in an instant as adrenaline surged through her. She struggled, twisting and turning, the sheets wrapping around her legs as she fought to scream. A heavy thigh swung over to trap her lower body.

"It's me." Luke's voice barely reached her as his warm breath caressed her neck. She stilled, chest heaving, gaze darting to the left. "I'm taking my hand away. Will you be quiet?" She nodded, her pulse still pounding in her ears.

He released her mouth and she took a huge gulp of air, almost choking. His hard body lay half on her, half on the guest bed she'd fallen into earlier. She could feel his breath on her cheek and goose bumps raced along her arms and legs.

"There's someone in the house," he whispered, making her pulse accelerate even more. No emotion tinged his voice. No fear, no excitement, nothing.

"Wh—"

He placed a finger over her lips. "Follow me. Stick close and do *exactly* as I say. Got it?"

She nodded.

"I mean it, Kate. Do what I say." His whispered voice took on a hard edge.

She nodded again as he stood and pulled her out of bed. Leaning close, he pressed his lips to her ear. "Don't make a sound. I'm going to try to get you out the back door. Run like hell to the neighbor's."

He glided to the closed bedroom door and eased it open a crack. Kate strained to catch any strange noise but could hear only the pounding of the blood in her ears.

"What about you?" she whispered, keeping her voice just as low.

"I can take care of myself."

Raising the barrel of his gun, Luke opened the door wider and grabbed her hand. He slid into the hallway, plastering himself against the wall. Kate did the same.

He scooted along the wall, pulling her with him, heading for the kitchen and the back door. He stopped. His hand tightened on her wrist and she winced.

She heard it, then. The groan of a floorboard. "In the living room," she whispered, knowing every creaking board in the place.

Luke nodded, his head turned in that direction. A faint gray from the coming dawn came from the direction of the living room.

After what seemed like an eternity, Luke finally moved, taking careful steps. They'd have to cross the small eating area to make it to the kitchen and the back door. If the intruder were in the living room, they'd be spotted.

Luke leaned down and whispered, "As soon as we get to the end of the hall, run through the dining room and out the back door. I'll make sure he doesn't get you."

She drew back and looked at the gun in his hand. Would he shoot the guy? She studied Luke's tense shoulders, the concentration on his face and the way he wielded that gun as if it were an extension of his arm.

Luke continued to scoot down the hall and Kate followed. One more step to go. Her heart rate increased and her breathing became shallow. Her legs turned to rubber and she doubted she'd make it two steps into the dining room before her knees gave out. She took a deep breath and tensed, ready for Luke's command to run.

A man's dark shape materialized in the doorway, so close Kate could smell the sweat on him, and she let out a little squeak at the same time Luke cursed.

Luke pointed the gun at the large form and reached out to flip the light switch on. Kate blinked, everything going white before her eyes could adjust.

Luke reached behind him and pushed Kate away milliseconds before a bullet slammed into the drywall next to her head. Another shot quickly followed the first.

Shock widened the man's eyes. A gurgling sound came from his open mouth while a dark stain spread over his shirt. Kate clapped her hands over her mouth and stared in horror as the stranger slumped to the ground, eyes wide open, unblinking.

"Come on." Luke grabbed her hand and skirted the dead man as he headed for the door, dragging her behind him. When they reached the cool night air, Kate gagged. Luke glanced at her over his shoulder and cursed. He grabbed her head and pushed it down as she lost the contents of her stomach in her petunias while tears streamed down her cheeks.

She'd just seen a man killed.

A dead man lay in her living room.

Luke had just *shot* a man.

Her stomach heaved again, but nothing came up. She wiped her mouth, but couldn't erase the bitter taste of bile. Her eyes watered, blurring the scene before her—flowers in full bloom, the street deserted except for pools of white light under the streetlamps. She expected her neighbors to come running from their houses upon hearing the gunshots, but nothing moved, the only sound the chirping of the crickets.

"Better?" Luke asked.

She shook her head.

He ran his hand down her arm and twined his fingers with hers. Goose bumps popped up on her skin. *Oh, God.*

"We gotta go, Kate." His urgent voice drifted through her brain. She stared at her house. Luke cupped her face and turned her head toward him, eyes hard. "Kate. Listen to me. We have to go." He spoke in a slow, deliberate cadence that penetrated her shock.

"We should call the cops."

"We can't." He looked around the dark, empty street. "Where are your car keys?"

She blinked.

Luke turned back to her. "Kate. Your car keys. Where are they? Come on, you gotta snap out of this."

She tried to focus on him, but everything went fuzzy. "In my purse."

"Where's your purse?"

How could he even *think* of leaving? He'd just killed a man! How could he be so calm? So in control?

He led her over to the front step and sat her down. "Stay here. Don't move." Then he disappeared. It was probably only minutes before he returned but Kate had lost track of time as she rocked back and forth. "Come on," he said, taking her arms and gently pulling her up. "Let's go."

He placed her into the passenger seat of her Jeep Wrangler and buckled her in. Then he walked around to the other side and slid into the driver's seat. Kate stared straight ahead as he backed out of her driveway and drove down the street.

The blank look in Kate's eyes scared the hell out of Luke. Her face was drained of color and she'd begun shaking. Shock. But he couldn't do a damn thing about it until he got them away from her house. He bit off a curse and hit the steering wheel with the heel of his hand, making Kate jump.

Nothing had gone right. He'd planned only to use her place as a temporary hideout to heal. Not put her in danger. So what had happened?

After lying in bed wide awake, unable to think of anything but Kate asleep in the next room, Luke had gotten up, needing to stretch his muscles, test his stamina.

Snoop.

He wouldn't lie, he'd wanted to check things out, learn what he could about this new Kate. So he'd prowled through her house and discovered things that disturbed him. He'd been standing in her living room trying to figure out what bothered him most when he'd heard a noise in the basement. He dropped to a crouch and half ran, half stumbled through the pain in his ribs to retrieve his gun. Then he'd gone to Kate. Thank God he'd listened to his gut because if he hadn't, both he and Kate would be dead instead of Hank Stuben, Suzanne Carmichael's bodyguard.

Luke checked his rearview mirror for a tail. Traffic was sparse, but just to be on the safe side, he exited the highway. A light blue compact was the only car that followed. Luke pulled up to a stop light where he waited in the left-hand turn lane, eyeing the compact. He turned right when the light switched to green, cutting across empty lanes. He needed to be careful and not attract the attention of the police, but he also needed to be certain they weren't being tailed. The little car turned left and Luke breathed a sigh of relief. He'd have to ditch Kate's car soon, before the cops discovered the body and started searching for the Jeep.

"You told me I was safe."

Her words were like a knife to his gut, the pain in his ribs nothing compared to the slice to his heart. And the look she shot him was worse, twisting that knife, tearing him apart on the inside, making his guilt spill out. He *had* told her she was safe and he'd been wrong. Dead wrong. Wasn't much he could say about that, was there?

"You're not an accountant, are you?"

He tightened his grip on the steering wheel. Her face was still pale and she'd wrapped her arms around her middle while she continued to stare straight ahead.

"Forensic accountant," he said.

"Whatever."

"No, I'm not."

"I didn't think so."

A stretch of silence followed while Luke tried to think what to say next, torn between telling her everything and keeping his secrets to himself. She deserved to know, yet he'd sworn an oath of confidentiality. Caught between a rock and a hard place. Not a feeling he particularly enjoyed.

"So what are you?" she asked, still refusing to look at him.

He sighed, checked his mirrors, changed lanes, all while trying to find the right answer and dealing with the fact that the government he'd very nearly given his life for had apparently just turned on him.

"I have a right to know," she said, finally turning toward him. The bleak look in her eyes nearly killed him, but it also cemented his decision. She *did* deserve to know.

Once again he checked his rearview mirrors but no one followed them. "I'm an operative for the International Anti-Terrorist Task Force, or IATT, for short."

"And that means?"

Luke clutched the steering wheel with his left hand and the gearshift with his right. What he was about to tell her was top secret. There were ramifications for divulging this information. Information that only the highest military brass knew. However, apparently he and Kate were running for their lives from that same agency so maybe that made his oath null and void.

"The IATT was formed just after 9/11. The President instituted Homeland Security but quickly realized he needed something with a wider reach, something other than the CIA, Al Qaeda and the Taliban knew about." Luke paused but Kate didn't seem inclined to fill the silence, so he went on. "I, um. I go undercover into territories with known terrorist activity, gather intelligence... Do what needs to be done."

Still staring out the window, her fingers picked at the purple polish on her nails and he gave her the time she needed to understand what "do what needs to be done" meant.

"So what happened back there? At my house."

Either she didn't want to think about the things he'd done, or her shocked mind hadn't processed that information yet. He wasn't about to force her, accepting the reprieve for what it was. "Look, Kate. I'm sorry. I really believed you were safe. No one knew of our connection except my boss." He had to get his apology out of the way first, before they could move on. From his calculations, and from what he remembered of the Northern

Kentucky area, he had about twenty minutes to convince her to go on the run with him.

"Your boss," she repeated with that dead inflection. "So that means your boss sent a man to kill you?"

Even in her shocked state, she was sharp. "Apparently."

Traffic was starting to get heavy, rush hour just beginning. It would make it harder for him to spot a tail but easier to blend in and lose one as well. He glanced at his watch and wondered how much time they had before someone discovered Stuben's body. It all depended on if the neighbors heard the gunshots.

"Why would your boss want you dead?" Kate asked. This time he heard a bit of inflection in her voice and when he glanced over, noted the color was returning to her cheeks. She sat up straighter and pushed her hair out of her eyes.

"I don't know," he answered honestly. "But I intend to find out."

She nodded, and another silence fell, this one thick with tension. Luke flipped on his turn signal and merged onto the entrance ramp.

Kate leaned forward and looked around. "We're going to the airport?" A hint of panic tinged her voice and he reversed his earlier thought. He'd rather have the bland tone rather than panic. He didn't need a panicked woman right now.

"Not exactly." He turned right when the light changed to green, pulled into a liquor store and parked under a sign shaped like a beer bottle. Off to their left, a jet seemed to hang suspended in the air, its nose pointed upward. Luke yearned to be on that jet, flying away from here with Kate beside him. No worries. No past that kept them apart.

He turned off the engine and cranked the window down to let the humid August air blow in. From here, he had a perfect view of long-term parking. A glance at his watch told him they had a bit of time so he settled in.

Kate watched the jet for a moment, then turned to him. Her eyes were still a bit glazed, but he could tell the shock was wearing off. "What now?" she asked.

"Now we wait. And talk."

She didn't settle back in her seat like he had, but sat poised at the edge, ready to run. Her gaze bounced around the parking lot and the long-term parking across the street. She paused when she saw the stand of trees to her right.

"Don't."

She jumped and looked at him. "Don't what?"

"Don't run."

"I wasn't—"

"And don't lie."

She bit her lip and looked away. The heavy air stirred but did nothing to cool them off. Before prowling her house, Luke had found his jeans, washed and folded, on her dresser. His shirt had been ruined so he'd rummaged in her closet, coming out with a man's white dress shirt. Now, for something to do and to give himself time to think, he rolled up the sleeves. He hadn't wanted to think why she had a man's shirt in her closet. He told himself it was none of his business.

"Are you married?"

The question startled him and he swung around to stare at her. "Hell, no!" he blurted out. "Why would you ask that?"

She shrugged. "It's just... After you left, I wondered. You hear about that. Men who have a wife and a girlfriend and manage to keep them apart."

He looked down at the sleeve he was rolling. "I'm not married," he said again. He'd wondered what she'd thought all these months, agonized over the pain and grief he'd caused her.

But his need to know hadn't been enough to return. He'd had his reasons but now he began to wonder if they'd been selfish or for her own good as he'd tried to convince himself.

He dropped his arm and stared through the windshield. "I owe you an explanation."

"Yeah. You do."

He swallowed. He could do this. He could tell her what happened. He didn't have to go into detail. Just tell her enough so she'd understand and convince her she needed to throw her lot in with him. But still, it took him a minute to gather the courage and to find the words he'd never really spoken out loud before.

"I was sent to Peru." He paused. "I was sent to Peru because there'd been some terrorist activity down there. A group called People of Light. *La Gente de la Luz.*" He whispered that last to himself though he knew Kate could hear him. The memories he kept locked away pushed at his mind but he wouldn't let them free.

"H-how long were you there?" she asked.

"Three months." He couldn't tell her the rest. Not yet, maybe not ever.

Movement in the long-term parking had him glancing at his watch. They were out of time. He turned to Kate, draping his arm over the back of her seat and hiding a wince when his ribs protested. "Look, Kate, I know I ruined whatever chance we had together. I know I have no right to ask you this, but I'd like you to trust me."

Her eyes narrowed but he kept going, hoping if he talked enough, the right words would come. "I don't deserve your trust. I know that. I accept that. But what happened at your house, it's not good. My boss is after me for reasons I can't even begin to figure out. She's..." How to describe Suzanne? "She's

43

powerful. I'd feel better if you came with me. So I can protect you."

An incredulous look crossed her face and he held up his hand, needing to say his piece. "I know I haven't done a good job of that so far, but I can do it. It's what I'm trained for. Come with me, please." His voice cracked on the please. He didn't want to leave her behind, and if she didn't voluntarily decide to come with him, he honestly had no idea what he would do.

"Why don't you call the police?" she asked.

"Because this is beyond the police."

"No one's that powerful, except maybe the president of the United States."

He kept his mouth shut and Kate's eyes went a little wider. "Are you saying the president of the United States is after you?"

"No." But close.

She glanced uncertainly at the parking lot attendants, biting her bottom lip once again. "If I don't go with you, what will you do? Where will you go?"

"It's probably best you don't know that."

"What will happen to me?"

He didn't know how to answer that question without scaring her, then decided maybe a little bit of fear would help his situation. "I don't know, Kate. Someone tried to kill me back there and he wouldn't have left you alive as a witness. The only thing I can guarantee is that you'll be safer with me than without me." He paused. "I need to know. Are you coming or not?"

Chapter Four

Kate wanted to close her eyes and pretend none of this had happened. There wasn't a dead man lying in her living room. She wasn't sitting in her car with Luke after he'd killed the dead man lying in her living room. It was all a dream. A nightmare.

But it wasn't. Luke *had* returned and killed a man, but that almost paled in comparison to what he was asking now. She rubbed at her aching temples, hoping she wasn't getting a migraine when her migraine medication was at home with the dead guy.

On top of that was this horrible sense of betrayal. She'd lived with Luke for nearly a year, given him everything she had to give, only to learn they'd been living a lie. The concept was so overwhelming it made her head hurt.

"Kate?"

She dragged her gaze back to his, took in the light sheen of sweat on his face, the circles under his eyes, the tightness around his mouth that told her he was in pain. And despite the betrayal and the deception, she actually considered going with him.

"What are you going to do?" she asked. "What plan do you have?"

"Find out what happened back at your house. Figure out why someone wants me dead."

Her gaze skittered over his body and his arm held protectively over his bruised ribs. "It's nothing I haven't lived through before," he said, apparently reading her mind.

His words were a reminder that he'd lived a life she'd been unaware of, that he'd deliberately lied to her for months while professing he loved her.

"I need an answer, Kate."

She closed her eyes as her heart began to race again. An image of that man sliding to the floor, a bullet in his chest, played over and over in her mind. *No, no. Calm down, Kate. You're with Luke.*

"Please," he whispered.

The please pushed her over the edge from victim to accomplice and sealed her fate. But if she were truthful she knew she couldn't go back to her house, especially with the person who'd ordered Luke's death still out there.

"All right, I'll go with you."

His shoulders sagged and he wiped the sweat off his brow. "Thank you."

"It doesn't mean I trust you, Luke. I don't know if I can ever trust you again."

He paused as he reached for the keys in the ignition. "I know," he said.

They pulled up to the long-term parking lot at shift change. Inside the booth, two men talked to each other, barely glancing at her while they handed Luke the ticket. Luke drove around the parking lot until he pulled into a space between two minivans. He twisted around and rummaged in the back seat, plopping her purse and a pair of white Keds in her lap.

"Where'd you get these?" she asked, staring down at the

items that seemed so ordinary in an extraordinary situation.

"I snagged them when I went back in the house for your purse." His gaze skimmed the running shorts and tank top she'd worn to bed the night before. "I should have grabbed clothes but there wasn't time. Put the shoes on."

While she placed her foot on the dash and tied her shoe, Luke put her sunglasses on her nose and came up with an old denim ball cap she kept in the Jeep for those sunny days when she drove with the top down.

"Put this on and wait right here. I'll be back."

"Wait." She reached out and grabbed his arm as she tucked her hair up in the cap with the other hand. "Where are you going?"

"I'm not leaving the parking lot, promise." He slid from her grasp and disappeared.

The long-term shuttle from the airport pulled in, disgorging a load of senior citizens wearing Hawaiian shirts. They broke apart with a lot of waves, kisses, hugs and laughter. Why couldn't she ever be that happy? Why couldn't she live a life that allowed her to step off a bus from paradise and go home to nothing more tragic than a few dead plants?

Luke's head popped up at her window and she jumped, her heart slamming into her throat. "Geez, you scared me."

He opened the door and held out his hand. "Come on, we don't have much time."

A boxy SUV idled behind them, keys in the ignition.

Luke opened the driver's side door. "I need you to drive."

"Huh?" She looked from the car to him and back, digging her heels in. They were *not* going to steal a car. No way. She wouldn't do it. She'd done some pretty horrible things in her life, but never grand theft auto.

He waved her in with an impatient swipe of his hand, his gaze going to the senior citizens now climbing in their own cars. "In. Get in. Drive."

Kate's gaze swung between the senior citizens, the men in the booth and the SUV.

"Trust me, Kate."

Her gaze focused in and out, that veil of numbness descending once again. Two days ago her life was finally, finally back on track, then whammo, Luke showed up and all hell broke loose.

"Get in, Kate."

She closed her eyes, but all she saw was the orange flash of a gun and the crumpled form of a stranger. Luke had saved her life. She didn't know why and she certainly hadn't discovered the circumstances surrounding all this, but he *had* saved her life. Decision made, she climbed in. Luke walked around the hood of the car, and climbed in the passenger side.

Kate grabbed onto the steering wheel. For a blinding second, her old fear came rushing back. In her mind she heard the squeal of tires. The grinding metal. Laura's screams, then her silence. Kate clutched the wheel until her knuckles turned white, stared at her white knuckles until they blurred, hearing it all over again as it raced before her eyes, stealing the breath from her lungs, immobilizing her.

She could do this. *She could do this.* She hadn't had this type of panic attack in months. Granted it'd taken that long to get behind the wheel again, but she'd overcome her fears. Or so she thought. Taking deep breaths she shoved the memories to the far reaches of her brain, and attempted to center herself like her counselor taught her.

"The ticket's above the visor." Amazingly enough the deep timbre of Luke's voice helped wrench her from her fears and she opened her eyes. "Pull up to the gate and pay, then drive away," he said as he made a visual search of the parking lot.

She threw the car in drive and with shaking hands, pulled into line behind the senior citizens.

She could do this.

The hours passed in a blur as endless expanses of highways merged. She probably should be keeping track of where Luke was going, what highways they'd been on, but her mind was on other things and her head pounded with a migraine. She was beginning to doubt this decision to go with Luke. She wished she'd had more time to think it over. Or maybe she wished she'd had more time to change her mind.

She felt like the world's biggest idiot. The man had conned her royally, lied to her even while he told her he loved her. *So the minute he shows up on your doorstep you lose your good sense?* Disgusted with herself, she turned to stare out the side window but the bright sun made her wince and she looked down at her hands, at the purple polish nearly picked off.

If she'd had time to think, to draw a breath without Luke pushing her for a decision, she would have thought of her job. She couldn't afford to lose it. Of course, the world was full of bars so she'd find another one, but that wasn't the point. The point was that once again Luke had walked in and turned her life upside down. Only this time she knew him for the liar he was.

Yet every time she closed her eyes, a dead man looked at her, shock marking his face, dark blood oozing from a hole in his chest. The same man Luke had killed had taken a shot at her and would have hit her if Luke hadn't shoved her out of the way. This time the tremors wouldn't stop and she shook, her teeth chattering, sending agonizing shards of pain through the left side of her skull.

She owed him. If nothing else, she owed Luke for saving her life. Of course, her life wouldn't have been in danger if he hadn't shown up. She just didn't know what to believe anymore. She wanted to go home, to curl up in her bed with the blinds closed and sleep the migraine away. But there was no going home. Not anymore.

Her eyes closed and, thankfully, she saw nothing behind her eyelids but bright bursts of light.

"Kate?" Concern laced Luke's voice. Her head ached and the muscles in her neck hurt. "Kate?" He shook her shoulder. The move jostled her head and she cried out. Her stomach rolled and she panicked as bile climbed up her throat.

The car accelerated. Horns honked before Luke pulled the vehicle to a smooth stop. The driver's side door opened, then slammed shut and Kate groaned. Her door opened and Luke's hands circled her waist, lifting her out of the truck. He made it to the side of the road just in time. She gagged, but nothing came up. She had emptied her stomach earlier, after the man had been murdered.

"Open your eyes, Kate."

She shook her head, wincing at the needle stabs of pain. "Can't. Migraine."

Mere feet away, cars roared past. Something larger, probably a semi, rumbled by. Birds chirped. Every sound seemed magnified, as if it originated inside her skull. The SUV idled behind her, heat radiating off the hot rubber tires, coating her in sweat.

Something cool was shoved into her hand. "Drink," Luke

commanded.

The ice-cold water slid down her parched throat as she eagerly guzzled it. Luke pried her fingers off the plastic bottle with one hand and held her up with the other. "Can you make it a few more miles to a hotel?"

Throbbing pain shot from her left eyebrow to her ear and down her neck making it impossible to speak. Hands lifted her up again. She draped her arms around Luke's neck, leaned her head against his broad chest and kept her eyes closed.

"Just hold on a little longer, Katie. I'll get us to a hotel room and take care of you." He placed her gently in the passenger seat and Kate sighed.

I'll take care of you.

Luke left Kate in the car while he ran into the hotel to reserve a room. He'd wanted a hotel a little more off the beaten path, but time and luck had worked against him. What would he do if her migraine didn't go away? He couldn't take her to a hospital and leave that sort of paper trail for Suzanne to follow.

He registered under the name Jay Lang and paid cash, then hurried back to the stolen SUV. Kate sat in the passenger seat, eyes closed, head lolling on the headrest. He never knew she suffered from migraines. They'd been together for almost a year! What other things didn't he know about her?

Even as he opened the passenger door and touched her arm, he realized the irony of that thought, considering most of their relationship had been a lie on his part. "Kate? Can you get out?"

She opened her eyes, groaned and snapped them closed again. He didn't want to carry her, afraid it would attract too much attention. A few moments later, she swung her legs out of the car and cracked open an eye. He reached inside and fished

51

out her sunglasses, gently placing them on her nose.

"Can you walk?"

She nodded and stepped out. Together, moving slowly, they made it up the outside stairs, Luke supporting most of Kate's weight by wrapping an arm around her waist. He unlocked and opened the hotel room door and led Kate in. She crawled onto the bed and lay on her stomach, arms tucked beneath her. Luke crouched beside her, took off her sunglasses and brushed her hair away from her face. "What can I get you?"

"Just need...sleep."

Her pale face under the honey tan gave her an air of vulnerability that tugged at him, pulling every protective instinct out of him. Who was he kidding? He'd felt protective towards her from the moment he'd first seen her. That was why, after Peru, he never returned. He couldn't afford to feel that way again—it hurt too much. He stood and paced the room. What had he been thinking, returning to her?

Kate breathed evenly, her lips parted, her face relaxed. Every survival instinct screamed at him to get out, to keep moving. But he couldn't leave, not with Kate like this. Besides, for the past several hours, the pain from his own injuries had begun to drag him down. He needed sleep too, yet he was fully aware he wouldn't get any. Not with Kate so vulnerable beside him and a stolen car out front telegraphing his location to anyone smart enough to look.

He sat on the other bed, pulled his feet up and plumped the pillows behind him. Grabbing the TV remote, he mindlessly surfed the channels.

Suzanne Carmichael sent Hank Stuben to kill him. Why?

Too restless to sit, he stood and paced to the window, cracking the curtains open and peering out, checking the parking lot. What was her game? What was her next move?

Kate stirred and Luke glanced at her over his shoulder. He sat in the chair next to the bed and tunneled his fingers through his hair. He'd been responsible for saving people's lives before. For getting diplomats, soldiers and average citizens out of some sticky situations. But none of those people had meant anything to him. They were just a job, a mission.

Not Kate.

Despite the year and a half spent apart, despite what he'd repeatedly tried to tell himself, Kate was his life. He'd die before he let anything happen to her.

He scrubbed his hands down his face and watched her sleep. He'd known what she'd been thinking in the car. She regretted her decision to come with him. She'd probably thought about the year they'd spent together and the lies he'd told. The lies had been necessary, mandatory even, but she wouldn't understand that, nor did he expect her to. She'd said she would go with him, but he knew he had an unwilling accomplice.

He stood once again and walked the length of the room, then made a return trip, his head bent, his mind jumbled with too many questions and not enough answers. He grabbed the remote and surfed the channels again, looking for a news network. *Know thy enemy.* He thought he'd known Suzanne pretty well. Now he was beginning to wonder.

He found CNN and turned the volume up enough to hear but not wake Kate.

"...killed Lucas Barone, a member of the CIA..." Eyes glued to the television, legs suddenly weak, he sank down on the bed. "Once again, police are looking for this woman." A picture of Kate with a neon pink streak in her long hair, wearing a flowing skirt that reminded him of the hippies in the sixties and a white peasant blouse that looked handmade, popped on the screen.

"Katherine McAuley. Eighteen months ago, Barone broke off his relationship with McAuley. There is speculation that McAuley shot Barone in revenge."

Luke closed his eyes and groaned.

"Police warn people not to approach her and to call your local authorities if you spot her. Once again, police are looking for this woman—"

Luke aimed the remote at the TV and turned it off. He sat in the quiet room, listening to Kate's breathing and the low hum of the air conditioner. What the hell just happened? Apparently, Suzanne had worked her magic and the police thought the dead man in Kate's house was him. Now every law enforcement officer in the country would be on the lookout for Kate.

If Luke wasn't so furious, he'd admire Suzanne's machinations and the way she'd so easily manipulated the situation to her advantage. *Don't go for him, go for his one weakness*, she would think. Well, that certainly sealed the deal with Kate. She had no choice now. She had to stay with him. He was the only one who could keep her safe.

He needed to talk to Suzanne, to discover whatever he could, but he couldn't do it from his cell phone or the phone in the hotel room. A quick glance at Kate confirmed she still slept. She'd never know if he left for a while. Just a few minutes. Enough time to get to a pay phone, make a call and collect a few necessities. He grabbed his keys, and with one more long look at Kate, decided she was safe for the time being, and left the room.

At a pay phone a few blocks away, he punched in a series of numbers that would send his call to a relay station. On the other end, a round of clicks connected him. After a long beep, he punched in more numbers, effectively scrambling his call to Suzanne. It wasn't foolproof—eventually she'd be able to trace the call—but it'd take longer than usual, and she'd find only a pay phone alongside a divided highway in a busy section of Knoxville, Tennessee.

Foot tapping on the cracked pavement, he studied the weeds growing up the side of the small booth and held the phone tight to his ear, hearing only the roar of blood through his veins.

"Hello?"

"Suzanne."

"Lucas."

She didn't sound surprised to hear from him. Raw fury erupted inside him, but years of training taught him to ignore his feelings.

"I assume you've heard about Hank." Her voice held no emotion, nothing to indicate the dead man meant anything to her.

"Considering I'm the one who killed him, I heard."

She laughed, a deep throaty sound he'd heard hundreds of times but had never sent chills up his spine like it did now. "Kate killed him, Lucas. Or, rather, Kate killed *you*."

"What's your game, Suzanne?"

"Come in and all the charges against Kate will be dropped. Run, and she will be among America's most wanted."

"Why?"

A pregnant pause followed his question. "You don't know?"

Ah, he'd surprised her. She thought he knew more than he did. So what was he supposed to know? "I want to hear it from you."

"That's so like you, Lucas. Cautious to the bone. Come in."

"You're dealing with the wrong person here. Watch your

back, Suzanne."

"Are you threatening me?"

Was it a federal offense to threaten a presidential candidate's wife? He assumed it didn't matter since dead people couldn't make threats. "Yes."

She chuckled. "We can wrap this up if you'd just come in. Show us you're still alive, that your Katie didn't kill you, and she'll walk away."

"Why do I get the feeling *I* won't walk away?"

"You're a very perceptive man, Lucas Barone. I always liked that about you. What's that saying?" she asked. "Oh, yes. You can run, but you can't hide. I'll find you and then what will happen? Poor Katie will be arrested for your murder. And you? Well, let's just say those murder charges won't be falsified after all. Ciao, Lucas."

The line went dead.

Chapter Five

Kate opened her eyes to find Luke lying on the other bed, his head propped on one hand, staring at her.

For a moment, in her sleep-addled mind, time seemed to stand still, then rush backward toward happier, more carefree times. To a place where life had been about as perfect as she could have imagined.

What happened to the man she'd fallen in love with? The guy who'd laughed and loved with her? The man she had known would have never killed someone, then run, stealing a car in the process.

Or would he? How much did she really know of Lucas Barone?

"How's your migraine?" he asked.

"Better." She rolled to a sitting position and scooted to the edge of the bed. He sat too. They were so close their knees almost touched as he reached for her hand, held it between his.

He studied her fingers. "How's the painting going?"

She went still, her mind on alert at the cautious yet probing tone in his voice. "F-fine."

"I couldn't sleep last night, so I wandered around your house."

She tried to pull away but he held tight. "Luke, please—"

"—And I noticed something, but didn't realize until right now what that something was." She tugged again but Luke's hold was firm. "When we were...together, you always had paint under your fingernails."

"Luke—"

"Why don't you have paint under your nails, Kate?"

"Soap and water." This time when she tugged, he let go.

"Bull." The one word dropped like an undetonated bomb between them. He was challenging her, but she didn't rise to the bait. Instead she stood.

"I think," she said slowly, "that you lost all right to ask me anything."

"You know how to hit where it hurts, don't you?"

"Yeah, well, I learned from the best."

"I never meant to hurt you."

She laughed, the sound harsh and disbelieving. She found it hard to battle down the months' worth of pain welling up inside her as she turned to look at him. "Then I'd hate to see what happens when you do mean to hurt me."

"I would never intentionally hurt you, Kate. You have to believe that."

"What time is it?" she asked in a bid to change the subject.

"Going on nine." He stood and stretched, the muscles in his back pulling his shirt tight and delineating each rock-hard plain and valley.

Kate turned away. She didn't need this...this attraction. "I need a shower."

"Go clean up, then we need to talk."

She shook her head, relieved the motion didn't send pain shooting through her skull. "No way, Barone. I'm hopping off this weird merry-go-round. You go on without me."

"I can't do that, Kate."

The look he sent her made her pause. "Why?"

He grabbed the TV remote that had been sitting on his bed and turned the TV on. The drone of a female reporter's voice filled the silence. "Police are looking for this woman." A picture of Kate flashed up on the screen. "Katherine McAuley. McAuley is accused of murdering Lucas Barone in her home early this morning—" He hit a button and the television went dark.

Kate stared in horror at the blank screen and sank to the bed. "Oh...my...God."

Luke watched her carefully. "Every cop out there has your description and they've been told you're dangerous."

She stared at him, her mind as blank as the television screen. "What have you done?" she whispered.

He winced, his gaze sliding away from hers then coming back, filled with even more regret than before. "I didn't do this." He waved toward the now-silent television. "I swear, Kate, I didn't do this."

Stunned, she bit her lip to keep from sobbing. If she cried, she'd lose all control and right now she needed control. She reached for the remote Luke had tossed on the bed and turned on the TV. Apparently Luke's death was the top story because the woman was still talking about it, as old pictures of Kate and Luke flashed on the screen.

"—speculation is that McAuley shot and killed Barone when he showed up eighteen months after breaking off their relationship. Close friends of McAuley say she was bitter at the unexpected breakup and had threatened to do Barone harm if she ever saw him again."

She stared slack-jawed at the screen. "I *never* said anything like that."

Her face flashed on the screen. "Once again, police are looking for this woman, Katherine McAuley, for the murder of—"

Luke gently plucked the remote from her hand and turned the TV off.

"Why are you doing this to me?" she asked, without looking at him.

He sighed, and from the corner of her eye, she saw him run a hand through his hair. "Kate, you need to listen. I didn't do this, but someone did. You have to trust me to get us out of this."

"Us? You're dead. There is no us. Just me. Wanted by the police." Oh, God. She closed her eyes against the panic closing in on her. Luke touched her arm but she jerked away, her eyes flying open. "We'll go to the police," she said, ignoring the desperation in her tone. "We can prove I didn't kill you and this will all be cleared up."

His lips thinned even as he shook his head. "There's still the dead body in your living room. A body I killed. And the person who did this, who fed the media this information, she won't stop just because I show up."

The small spurt of hope inside her died. "Who is this person?" He seemed to fear the mastermind behind this and that scared her. Because in the last twenty-four hours she'd seen a side of Luke Barone she'd never seen before. A hardened warrior who shouldn't be scared of anyone.

"Her name is Suzanne Carmichael."

Kate stared at him, the name ringing all kinds of bells. "Suzanne Carmichael," she repeated. "The same Suzanne Carmichael whose husband is running for president of the United States? The same Suzanne Carmichael who people say is going to be the next First Lady? *That* Suzanne Carmichael?"

"I know it sounds...strange."

She shook her head. "No, not strange. Bizarre. Off the wall, maybe. Weird. Yes, definitely weird." She was blabbering but couldn't seem to stop herself. None of this made sense and she began to wonder if maybe Luke was making it all up. Maybe something terrible had happened to him during those missing months and he'd lost his mind or something.

But then she remembered the newscast and her picture flashed for all the world to see. No, he hadn't made this up. As bizarre as the Suzanne Carmichael story was, it would be even more bizarre for Luke to fake his own death and blame her. So that lead to one question. Who had identified the intruder's body as Luke and why?

"You better tell me everything."

Luke studied her for a moment, looking concerned and chagrined all at the same time. "Suzanne and I go way back. We...worked together."

"For this IATT?"

Luke nodded. "Suzanne is my boss."

"The boss who sent the man to kill you?"

"His name was Hank Stuben."

Somehow, knowing the man's name seemed worse, because it made his death all the more real. He had a name, he'd lived somewhere, had friends. "Luke, I'm sorry. I can't... This is all so surreal."

"I know. I understand."

"So Suzanne Carmichael sent a man to kill you and now claims that man is you and I'm the one who killed you. Why?"

"Suzanne is good, Kate. She knows my Achilles' heel, the one thing I'd die to protect."

She wrinkled her nose. "And what's that?"

He stared at her, those cool gray eyes burning into her. "You. I'd die to protect you."

She surged off the bed and took a hurried step back, almost tripping in her haste to get away. Her hand flew up as if she could physically stop his words. "No! Damn you, Luke Barone, don't do this!" She bit back another curse. "I'm over this," she said, more to convince herself than anything. "I thought you had died. I called your sister, your office, the police. I did everything I could to find you." Locked inside for so long, the words she'd been holding back suddenly flowed out and it felt good to let them go. By the color draining from Luke's face, it didn't look like he wanted to hear what she had to say, however. Too bad, she couldn't stop them even if she wanted.

"Everyone, including the police, said you were a grown man, that you could leave me if you wanted. They said that maybe you wanted out of our relationship. I knew they were wrong." She swiped at something tickling her cheeks only to discover tears. "Then your secretary quit answering your phone and suddenly the number didn't work anymore. And then Laura and the ba—" She stopped suddenly. Luke's gaze sharpened in interest but she looked away.

"What about Laura?" he asked.

Kate closed her eyes. An all-too-familiar ache started deep inside at hearing her sister-in-law's name. "Th-then I believed," she whispered into the silence. "Finally, I realized you weren't ever coming back."

Luke muttered a string of words in another language and took a step forward, but Kate stumbled back and he stopped. They faced each other for the longest time, so much unsaid between them, so many months of separation that could never be explained.

Some of the fight seemed to go out of him and he turned away. "We need to get going before somebody recognizes the car out front."

He waved to a fast food restaurant cup sitting on the dresser as he pulled clothes out of a plastic bag. "I went out earlier and got some stuff," he said without looking up. "I didn't know if you had one of those migraines that needed caffeine."

She grabbed the now-warm drink and took a grateful sip through the straw. "Caffeine helps. Thanks."

He crossed his arms over his chest and studied her. "I didn't know you suffered from migraines."

"I didn't always."

His gaze sharpened. "When did they start?"

"Recently."

"How recently?"

She slid past him to walk into the bathroom.

"How recently, Kate?"

"About eighteen months ago." She glanced over her shoulder at Luke who looked like she'd just conked him on the head with a mallet.

"My God, Kate."

"They're better now. I don't get them as often." She paused. "Only when I'm stressed."

He opened his mouth as if to say something, but only a sigh escaped. He ran a hand through his hair, causing the short tawny strands to stick up. "I'm sorry."

"For what?"

"For leaving. For putting you through that."

"It has nothing to do with you." The memories pushed at her, but she ignored them. It was all so complicated. Everything was intertwined. It was like those braided rugs, no beginning, no end, nothing to separate the strands. Luke's desertion. Laura. If you pulled one, the whole thing would fall apart.

Luke stared at her for another minute and it seemed as if he wanted to say something. Instead he picked up a bag. "I asked the pharmacist what over-the-counter medicine would help a migraine. He recommended these." Bottles tumbled from the bag.

Relieved he didn't demand an explanation on what exactly had sparked her migraines, she said, "Thanks, but the caffeine should do the trick."

He began emptying bags, putting clothes in a duffel bag he'd apparently bought as well. Toiletries, snacks, a pocketknife, more bottles of pills, some gauze and bandages and anti-biotic ointment went in with the clothes.

He held up a pair of scissors. "You'll need to cut your hair."

She backed up. "Uh-uh. No way."

He looked up from shoving clothes into the bag, his eyes hard. "Yes. You will. We don't have far to go, but with every Tom, Dick and Harry looking for you, we can't take chances."

No, she couldn't do it. Wouldn't do it. Kate fingered a hunk of long hair, her insides a quivering ball. She wouldn't look at Luke, but she could feel his eyes on her. Daring her to return to the person she'd been running from for months. She lifted her eyes, her gaze locked with his.

"What are you hiding from, Kate?"

"Other than the cops?" Everything. Herself. Who she'd been, what she'd become. What she hadn't become.

Twenty minutes later, she stared at herself in the bathroom mirror. Her old self. The self she'd tried to forget had existed.

She touched the blonde curls. He'd cut a good eight inches and the corkscrew curls sprang back, just the way he'd always liked it. The cut seemed to brighten her blue eyes and accentuate her cheekbones. With her face devoid of the dark makeup she'd taken to wearing, she looked... She turned away. To her, that person symbolized someone carefree. Someone who hadn't lost so much. Done something so horrible, so devastating...

"There's the Katie I know," Luke whispered behind her.

"Did you do this to hide me from the police or because you wanted a reminder of what I'd been?"

His gaze flickered over her hair. "Both."

Angry that he'd made her confront herself, she grabbed a hair band and wrapped her hair in a short ponytail.

"Here." Luke shoved a yellow bottle of fingernail polish remover at her. "Take the purple polish off."

She sighed and grabbed some tissues. *You're doing this to elude the police. When this is done you can return to your...* Disguise was the only word she could come up with to describe her former appearance.

When she emerged from the bathroom, Luke examined her with a critical eye. The denim shorts fit perfectly and reminded her of something she would have worn in her previous life. She'd pulled the red camper shirt over a white tank top and tied the ends over her midriff.

"Take your earrings out."

Her hand went to her ear. "What?"

"Your earrings. Take all but one pair out."

"Why are you doing this?" Anger mixed with tears and she blinked them away.

"So you don't get arrested," he said, his voice devoid of

emotion.

She removed the earrings.

Luke hiked the duffel bag over his shoulder and scanned the room, his granite gaze finally resting on her. "Ready?"

She took a deep breath and stared at the door. Suddenly, she didn't want to go out there. She wanted to stay safely tucked inside this hotel room while life passed her by.

She looked at Luke, at the hard, reassuring presence of him, at his rock-solid strength and his razor-sharp mind. Reality hit her broadside, almost bowling her over. She'd never make it on her own. Not in this world she was so unfamiliar with.

She took another deep breath. "Ready."

"Found it." Suzanne's administrative assistant rushed into her office waving a piece of paper in the air and smiling.

Suzanne looked up from the papers on her desk and frowned. "Found what?"

"Katherine McAuley's car." Jessica's voice lowered a notch.

The entire office was in an uproar over Lucas's "death", outraged that an operative had been killed so easily by none other than someone he should have been able to trust. Suzanne couldn't have been more pleased.

When the Cincinnati Police Department ran Stuben's fingerprints, red flags went up in Suzanne's department, as it did any time an operative's fingerprints were run. She'd intercepted the message and taken matters into her own hands. It hadn't been hard to pin Lucas's identity on Hank, then take the body home. Hank's family was scattered and didn't keep in touch and Suzanne simply told her staff Hank took some vacation time, all while his body was being cremated at a local funeral home. And she'd found early on that the media would believe just about anything if you looked sincere enough.

Jessica slapped the paper in front of Suzanne, a little out of breath. "Police found the car in a long-term parking facility at Cincinnati International Airport."

Suzanne sat back and grinned. *Ah, Lucas, how cunning you are.* She'd taught him well. The thrill of the chase raced through her. How long had it been since she'd matched wits with someone as cunning and deceptive as Lucas? "How'd they find it?"

Jessica sat on the edge of the chair across from Suzanne's desk, her eyes bright with excitement. "A man called the police reporting his car stolen. When the officers came to take the report, one of them recognized the description we put out for McAuley's vehicle."

"Were any other cars stolen from that particular lot?"

"None."

Suzanne tapped her fingernails on her desk. "So we have to assume Katherine stole it. Did you get a license plate number?"

Jessica leaned over and tapped the piece of paper. "Right here. Description of the vehicle and everything. Light tan, 1999 Chevy Blazer."

Suzanne stared at the paper and smiled. Her body hummed with the power, with the adrenaline, with the excitement of the game.

"Get the description to every police department in the country."

Chapter Six

Luke nudged a reluctant Kate out of the hotel room and closed the door behind them. Wrapping his arm around her waist, he led her down the long walkway to the car. "Act like you belong," he said. "If you look fearful and hesitant, people will notice."

She lifted her chin and leaned the long length of her body into his embrace. He tightened his hold on her not because he feared for her safety, but because he wanted to hold her. "If I'd known this is what it takes to get you in my arms—oomph. Ouch!"

She pulled her elbow out of his ribs. "You're enjoying this, aren't you?"

"No." He opened the rear passenger door of the Blazer and tossed in the duffel bag. He could honestly say he wasn't enjoying any of this. The only good thing to have come out of the situation was that Kate was back in his life. But he feared the cost was too high.

Kate looked around the nearly deserted parking lot. "I don't find this funny at all. You may not take this murder charge seriously, but I do."

He paused in unlocking the passenger door, his gaze snapping to hers. "Believe me," he said, twisting the key in the lock. "I'm taking this seriously. Whoever set me up and accused you of this murder will pay. Never doubt that." He opened the door, and she paused before climbing in. Luke watched her reaction closely.

She stared at the pencils and paper for a long while, her face expressionless. When he'd left eighteen months ago, Katherine McAuley was making a name for herself as the next up-and-coming artist. Her paintings were bringing in solid profits, enough for her to work at it full-time and not have to worry about making the mortgage payment. Her art had consumed her and now it didn't. The evidence, or lack thereof, had been all over her house.

Surely his leaving hadn't caused her to stop painting, had it?

He sighed and walked around to the driver's side where he climbed in and fired up the engine. "I checked out earlier, so we don't have to worry about that. We'll be on the road for about three hours." He waited until she climbed in, then put the car in drive and pulled out of the parking space. "What's the matter, Kate?"

"Where'd you get these?" She clutched the pad of paper and pencils in her hand.

"I picked them up in the school supply aisle of Wal-Mart. I know they're not as good as what you're used to, but I figured since you didn't have time to pack your own stuff, you needed something."

He was goading her, waiting for a reaction, something that would tell him what was going on in her mind. And it wasn't just about her art. There were other secrets Kate was keeping from him and they weighed heavily on his shoulders. He wanted to know all there was to know about her. What she'd done during the past eighteen months and where she'd been.

There had been a time, before he screwed up, when she

would have told him everything and it hurt more than he'd imagined that she wouldn't do it now. Of course there was that trust issue she'd warned him about.

Out of nowhere her words came back to him. *I called your sister, your office, the police.* As they'd done when she'd first said them, the words punched him in the gut, making his bruised ribs ache. He hadn't had a clue what to say then and still didn't now. *I'm sorry* just didn't seem to cut it.

She twisted around and placed the paper and pencils on the back seat.

"You okay?" he asked.

"Sure."

Liar. But he kept his mouth shut. Questioning her at this point would only push her farther away and he didn't need that right now.

They drove in silence for several miles with only the low hum of the tires and an occasional passing car to break the quiet. For something to do, Luke fiddled with the radio, tuning into an easy listening station. One with few commercial breaks and little news coverage. In the dark interior, the music created a romantic aura, and for the first time in eighteen months, Luke began to relax. Ironic, considering he was driving a stolen car and running from the law.

"So what happens next?" she asked.

"We get somewhere safe."

"You have a place in mind? Because I'm thinking nothing's safe right now."

"You're safe with me. Trust in me, Kate. I'll get us out of this."

She blinked, but her expression didn't give him hope that she'd ever trust him again. After Peru, he'd done everything he could to get Kate out of his system—volunteered for the worst, most dangerous missions, buried himself in other women, meaningless women. Women who left him empty and desolate. He'd given them up almost right away, because he'd found it more painful being with them than not being with Kate.

"I do," she whispered.

"You do what?"

"I do trust you."

Everyone, including the police, told me you left because you didn't want me anymore.

It was as if he were back in the Peruvian prison being tortured all over again. He couldn't even begin to imagine what Kate had been through. The confusion, the fear, the desperation. He, of all people, knew how useless it was to think in should haves. He should have told her the truth from the beginning. He should have contacted her after his release. Maybe even, he should have walked away from her that day at the art gallery and never introduced himself in the first place.

But should haves *were* a waste of time. He hadn't done any of those things and because he hadn't he would pay the price with the guilt he would carry for the rest of his life.

I knew they were wrong.

He winced. They hadn't been wrong. He'd stayed away not because he didn't want her anymore, but because he'd known she wouldn't want him.

"So, where are we going?" she asked, snapping him back to the present. To reality.

"I have a place on Catawba Lake in Tennessee. No one knows about it. We'll be safe."

"For how long?"

"Long enough to figure out what the hell's going on." His

anger returned at the thought of Suzanne's deception. To betray a fellow operative was tantamount to treason. She'd exposed him. Now he had to figure out why. What had he done to bring this down on his head? And Kate's. He could never forget that Kate was in this because of him.

Uneasy silence descended again as the miles continued to accumulate. Kate fought sleep, jerking her head up every time she dozed. Eventually she gave in and leaned her head against the side window. It gave him an opportunity to study her.

This was the Kate he knew, the Kate who'd pulled him through some horrific times. She didn't like the change he'd forced upon her, had been trying to hide from something by altering her appearance. What? What was Kate hiding from? What would make her stop painting? Her tortured eyes told him it was something inside, something she didn't want to face.

He reached over and touched a curl that had escaped her ponytail. He ran his knuckle down her cheek. *I knew they were wrong.* He would never forget those words or the resignation in her voice that, more than anything, told him that she now knew they had been right.

The night dragged on. Traffic became sparse. Luke kept the SUV five miles over the speed limit. He constantly checked the rearview mirrors. Every hour or so, he exited the highway and drove back roads, just in case. The three-hour time limit he'd given had already stretched into four and they still had about fifty miles to go.

Dawn had crested hours ago. His legs began to ache. Needing a break, he pulled into the next rest stop where semis were parked to the side, their running lights on, engines idling. A few other cars dotted the area.

Kate stirred and opened her eyes. "Where are we?"

"Somewhere in Tennessee." He loved watching her wake up. It had always been the best part of his day, seeing the blurry sleep in her eyes, then the recognition, the slow smile that spread across her face upon seeing him.

She stretched, arching her back and raising her arms over her head. "Mmmm. That felt good."

Luke turned away. "Need to use the bathroom?"

"Yup." She hopped out of the truck and waited for him to join her.

Before they parted at the bathrooms, Luke leaned over and kissed her temple. "Be careful."

Panic leapt into her eyes and she quickly glanced around. Luke nudged her with his shoulder. "Go. I'll be right here when you get out." Experience taught him he'd be in and out, his business done, well before Kate.

When he emerged, he immediately made a visual sweep of the rest area, looking for Kate. Unable to locate her, he leaned against the building, planting one foot against the cinder block wall and burying his hands in his jeans pockets. His gaze stopped on a deputy sheriff's car slowly cruising the lot.

Kate emerged from the bathroom and stopped short when she saw the cruiser. Luke could practically see the pulse jump in her neck as her gaze darted around until she spotted him.

He pushed away from the wall and sauntered toward her. Wrapping an arm around her waist, he pulled her trembling body close, leaned down and placed a kiss on the top of her head.

"Put your arm around my waist. Walk with me." She did as he said, her eyes glued to the cruiser. "Don't look at him. Look at me."

She swallowed and looked up at him. With his free hand,

he pulled her ball cap lower, hiding her panicked eyes. She licked her lips and he brought her in for a swift hug. "Just pretend he's not there."

"Easy for you to say. You're not wanted for murder."

"Shhh." No one was near enough to hear, but Luke knew from experience things like trees, bushes and buildings had ears. "I'm not dead yet."

She shuddered. "Don't say that."

"Say what?" The cruiser drove by. The deputy didn't glance up, didn't appear to have seen them.

"Don't say 'yet'."

He tried to determine what exactly her words meant.

They made it to the stolen SUV and Luke casually turned around to watch the cruiser. Had the cop noted the plate number? Had he written it down to run it? Hoping they wouldn't be caught by a routine plate check, he opened the car door. "Hop in."

She climbed in. Luke slammed the door shut and hurried, trying not to attract attention, to his side where he slid in and started the engine. He pulled away, accelerated smoothly down the entrance ramp and merged into traffic when all the while he wanted to stomp his foot down on the accelerator and race away.

Two cars behind, the deputy's cruiser entered the stream of traffic. Luke tightened his hold on the steering wheel.

Kate twisted around to look out the rear window. "Oh, God. He's following us."

"You don't know that."

She turned back and stared out the front windshield. "What else is he doing? Going for a Sunday drive?"

"He's driving the interstate. That's his job."

"He's following us."

Luke checked his speed and set the cruise control at two miles over the limit. He leaned his elbow on the door and his other wrist on top of the steering wheel. "Quit looking so panicked."

"I *am* panicked. I'm not trained for this...this sneaking around like you are."

The cruiser inched up a few car lengths, but remained a good thirty yards back.

And then suddenly it was behind them, and Luke held his breath, expecting the light bar to start flashing.

His gaze darted from the road in front of him to the rearview mirror and back to the road. The cruiser pulled even closer, almost riding his bumper. Luke flipped on his turn signal and drifted into the middle lane. If the cop wrote down the license plate number, the game was up and there really wasn't much he could do. Luke looked at the deputy in the side mirror just as the deputy picked up his radio and spoke into it.

The red and blue lights on top of the cruiser sprang to life. Luke let out his breath as his heart landed in his shoes. They'd been caught. He flipped on his turn signal again and attempted to merge into the far right lane. His mind raced, trying to figure out what to do now. Kate thought turning themselves in would solve everything. What he didn't tell her was that he had no proof he was Lucas Barone. He'd left all his identification at home when he took on Jay Lang's persona. So claiming he was Barone wouldn't work. Suzanne would still find them and they'd be in even more trouble than they were now.

The high-pitched whine of a siren yanked Luke's gaze back to the rearview mirror. The cruiser accelerated past and kept going. Hands shaking, Luke continued on, a wide smile playing across his face.

"Hot damn! We did it!" He slammed the palm of his hand on the steering wheel in elation.

"After you drink that pop and milkshake, we'll be making another pit stop."

Kate sucked the chocolate shake through the straw, her lips puckered around the white plastic. With a groan of pure animal frustration, Luke turned away.

In deference to the heat and humidity, Kate had shucked the camp shirt earlier. Now she wore only a tank top and shorts. The damp air had her hair springing into its natural curl and the smooth skin of her tanned thighs begged him to touch. It was becoming extremely difficult to sit next to her in the tight confines of the SUV and not remember what it had been like between them. More and more his mind kept drifting to the past and that wasn't a good thing. Not now, while they were on the run and definitely not when Kate didn't trust him with anything more than her safety.

She chomped on her burger while expertly maneuvering the big vehicle down the highway. After he finished his grilled chicken sandwich, Luke folded the paper wrapper and dropped it in the bag. Kate licked her fingers, balled up her wrapper and threw it on the floor at his feet.

"Okay. Now that I'm rejuvenated with food, you can tell me."

He gathered up her used napkins, cardboard French fry holder and straw wrappers and put them in the makeshift trash bag. "Tell you what?"

"Why Suzanne Carmichael's after you and how you came to work for her."

Luke placed the bag at his feet and stretched his legs, settling back in his seat. He folded his hands over his stomach and stared at the running lights of the truck in front of them. It'd been drilled into his head from the time he took his oath not to reveal anything about the IATT. He should at least feel guilty for telling Kate the agency even existed. At the most, he should feel shame, but he felt neither of those things. Relief, maybe, but that was it.

"How'd you get into the IATT?" she asked.

The truck in front of them changed lanes. Kate accelerated past and Luke checked the speedometer. "Take it easy, no more than five miles over the speed limit." She sighed, rolled her eyes and raised her foot off the gas. The SUV slowed, and Luke settled back down to think about his answer.

Not long after they'd met and he'd moved in with her, he'd told Kate about his childhood, how his parents had been struck by a semi and killed instantly. Luke's sister had been nineteen at the time and named guardian of nine-year-old Luke. With the pain of losing both parents so suddenly and having no father figure to control him, and a sister who didn't want him, Luke went over the edge. He started doing drugs at the age of twelve, stealing at fourteen.

"In high school, I was a hell-raiser," he said. "Always in trouble. My senior year, a buddy and I went four-wheeling in this pit the city dug for a lake in the hopes of bringing tourism to the area. It was a big mud hole. Dave and I were having a good time, ripping up the bottom of what would soon be the lake, generally causing a disturbance and being the bad kids everyone said we were. The four-wheeler hit a rock and overturned, pinning Dave underneath. He died."

Dave's death had been a turning point for him. Seeing his friend pinned under the four-wheeler, his neck at an odd angle, waiting those interminable minutes for the squad to get there, Luke had finally realized if he didn't change his life, he'd end up like Dave.

"I'm sorry about your friend," she said softly.

"I joined the Army after that. My sergeant saw something in me that others had seen but chalked up to bad blood. He referred me to the sniper division. Remarkably, I passed, then one thing led to another until Suzanne found out about me and recruited me."

"And now Suzanne wants you dead."

"Seems that way."

Kate reached for her milkshake and took a sip. "Why?"

"I don't know."

Both eyebrows rose this time. "You don't know? One minute she's your boss and the next she wants you dead?"

"That's about the sum of it."

"I don't buy it."

Neither did he.

"Tell me what happened the last time you saw her."

Luke took a sip of his own drink. "I was at a dinner party at the Carmichaels'. Every once in a while they'd invite some of the operatives if we were in town. They always kept it very small so our covers wouldn't be blown. People from the office and such."

"So what happened? What'd you do there?"

"I was bored out of my mind. Stepped outside for some air, saw Brad talking to someone, and not wanting to intrude, I went back in. Saw Suzanne, talked to her for a minute, then left."

Her brows drew together in a frown. "Hmmm. That sounds innocent enough. What happened next?"

"On the way home, I stopped at a bar and had a few drinks. When I got home, I noticed my security system had been disabled but by then it was too late. Two men dragged me inside and beat me."

But for the grace of God and a nightly patrol of his street that had spooked the thugs, Luke was still alive. He wouldn't tell Kate but he suspected he was supposed to have died in what would have appeared to be a burglary gone bad. He assumed Stuben had been sent to finish what the intruders had failed to do. What he couldn't figure out was why.

"So then what'd you do?"

"I had an escape plan. Something I'd put together a long time ago in case I needed to go on the run fast. That's where Jay Lang comes in. He's my alternate identity. I grabbed my new ID, some cash I'd stashed away, and ran."

"That's when you came to me?"

"Yes."

"Why me?"

Ah, and wasn't that the sixty million dollar question? Why Kate? Why return after all these years? Because he needed her?

He pointed up ahead. "Take the next exit and turn left."

She flipped on her blinker and merged onto the exit lane. It took a while for him to realize she'd gone silent. He'd been thinking about the party at the Carmichaels', wondering if Kate was on to something with that line of thought, but the silence pulled him from his thoughts and he turned to see her lips drawn down and furrows between her brows.

"What's wrong?"

She shrugged, then bit her lower lip. "Why?" she asked.

"Why what?"

"Why'd you lie to me all that time? Why couldn't you trust me with the truth?"

"It had nothing to do with trust. None of us were allowed to tell anyone what we did for a living. Even those who were married. The IATT is a secret organization by necessity. We fight the terrorists on a level the American public wouldn't understand."

She seemed to think about that as the silence stretched on and Luke tried to determine what question she'd hit him with next. "What are you thinking?" he finally asked.

She opened her mouth to say something, then closed it. Finally, she seemed to come to a decision. "I'm trying to figure out what was the lie and what was the truth in our relationship." She cut him a glance before turning her attention to the road ahead. "What was real and what was fake?"

He sucked in a breath that made his bruised ribs ache. The pain in her voice got to him, stabbed at his guilt. "Everything except what I did for a living was the truth," he said quietly.

"Our love?"

"God, Kate, I hate that you even have to ask. Our love was true. What I felt for you was true."

"Then why did you leave? And why didn't you come back?"

He turned to stare out the side window, not knowing how to answer without opening the holes inside him. "I'd been told I would be gone a few days, nothing more. I figured I'd call you once I got to Peru." It hadn't been strange for him to be called away at the last minute. In his fake life as a forensic accountant he was called away a lot and Kate had become used to it. Or at least she had seemed to.

"So why didn't you come back?" she whispered.

"Because I couldn't."

Chapter Seven

Kate wanted to ask more. Wanted to know if Luke had thought they could live the rest of their lives like that. Him going to a fake office, flying off to foreign countries to fight evil while she believed he was crunching numbers.

But Luke stopped the questioning by twisting around and grabbing the duffel bag off the back seat. He rummaged around in it, pulled a few things out, then began unbuttoning his shirt.

Kate shot him a startled glance. "What are you doing?"

"Changing."

"Why?"

"It's part of my disguise."

"What disguise?"

He pulled out a bright blue Hawaiian shirt with big lemon yellow pineapples all over it. "Keep your eyes on the road!" He grabbed the steering wheel and righted the drifting vehicle.

She snapped her attention back to her driving while he shrugged out of the white button down and pushed his arms into the Hawaiian shirt that was two sizes too big.

When he put his hands on the button of his jeans, Kate slammed on the brakes. Luke shot forward, throwing his hands out to catch himself on the dashboard. "What are you doing?"

"What are *you* doing?"

"I told you. Changing."

"Your *pants*?"

"Jeez, Kate, it's not like you haven't seen everything before." He pulled his gun from his waistband and placed it on the floorboard, then lifted his hips to shimmy out of the jeans.

Kate averted her eyes, her jaw set, her hands clenched around the steering wheel.

He shoved the jeans in the duffel bag and pulled the cargo shorts on, blousing the Hawaiian shirt over it and tucking his gun in the small of his back. Next he pulled down the visor and fixed his hair in the mirror, then snapped it shut. "Turn left up there."

Kate slowed, waited for traffic to pass, then turned left. She'd seen him barely dressed while he lay in her bed a few days ago, but Luke Barone nearly naked did something to her. She took another drink of her now-melted chocolate shake, just to put some moisture back in her mouth.

Per Luke's instructions, she stopped the Blazer behind what appeared to be a small neighborhood grocery store perched on the side of some back road. She climbed out of the truck. Luke met up with her and her jaw almost dropped.

He looked different. Yet the same. The overly large shirt added about twenty pounds to his lithe frame. He'd parted his hair in the middle and donned a pair of gold wire-rimmed glasses. She had to laugh at the white socks and sandals.

He smiled and grabbed her hand, walking her around to the front of the store. "Stay just inside the door. Don't say anything to anyone." He pulled open a wooden screen door and they both stepped into the dim interior.

The place was like an old-time grocery complete with wood floors and a musty smell. Luke left her at the entrance while he wound his way to the back where a teenage girl manned the register. She looked up, popped a big, pink bubble with her gum and smiled.

"Hiya, Mr. Reynolds."

"Hi, Carrie." He dipped his head, his voice coming out soft, almost embarrassed by the teenager's attention.

Right before her eyes Luke had transformed himself from an overly confident alpha male to a blushing, insecure, nerdy man. It made it all the more apparent that he wasn't the man she'd thought she'd known.

The cashier pushed some buttons on the old-time cash register and extracted a set of keys when the drawer opened. "Here ya go."

"Thanks." Luke took the keys and bobbed his head again as if he couldn't quite look the girl in the eye.

A tiny mewling noise drew Kate's attention downward. To the side of the door sat a box filled with kittens. A sign on the outside said *Free to a good home.* She sank to her knees and picked up a little fur ball. Immediately he nuzzled into her and she laughed. Another tried to climb up her leg but tumbled back down. She scooped that one up as well and held them both to her cheek, their soft fur reminding her of Picasso. Burying her face in the kitten's fuzz, she sniffed back the tears of homesickness and wondered what had happened to her cat. She played with the kittens while Luke purchased supplies for wherever they were headed.

"Ready?" He looked down at her with an odd expression.

She hugged the kittens to her a little tighter.

"Oh, no," he whispered, backing away, panic crossing his face. "No. No kittens."

"But they're free."

"I don't care. No way. Picasso and I don't get along. Why do you think that—" he motioned to the black and white ball of fur in her hand, "—one would be any different?"

She sighed and kissed the kitten on his nose. He mewled and batted at a stray curl.

Luke muttered a few expletives and placed the bags of food on the floor. "One." He held up his finger. "Just one."

"Really? I can have one? Oh, Lu—"

He placed his finger over her lips. "Shhh. No real names here," he whispered.

"Thanks," she whispered back.

"I must be insane," he mumbled and headed to the cash register where he purchased kitty litter, food and bowls. At the last minute, he threw in a toy mouse.

Kate smiled and hugged the kitten closer to her.

"Oh, Mr. Reynolds," Carrie said when he turned away with his new purchases. "I forgot to tell you, Sheriff Callahan's looking for you."

Kate froze. The kitten shifted.

Luke didn't even blink as he walked away. "Thanks, Carrie. Act natural," he said under his breath as he passed her, snagging the other bags on his way. "You look like you've seen a ghost."

Kate hurried after him. "But the *sheriff's* looking for you," she stage whispered as she tried to keep up with his long strides.

"I know."

"Isn't that bad?"

"Under some circumstances, yes." He put the groceries in the back seat and climbed in the driver's side while Kate got in the passenger side. Snuggled against her chest, the kitten cleaned his paws.

"So what are you going to do about it?"

"I'm going to get you to my place, ditch the stolen car and figure out why Suzanne wants me dead. That's what I'm going to do about it."

Kate wanted to argue. She had a bad feeling about this. But the expression on Luke's face told her he wasn't going to talk about it. Besides, the only thing he'd probably say was, *trust me.*

She settled back in her seat and decided by this point she didn't have any other choice but to trust him.

"Oh, how cool is *that?*" Kate stepped back as Luke pulled branches and leaves off a camouflage-painted three-wheeler. "Can I drive?"

"No."

"Please?"

"No."

She huffed, blowing a curl out of her eye. "You're no fun."

He shot her an amused glance, a corner of his mouth tilting in a smile. "What, you don't think it's been fun stealing a car, then racing through two states with the cops hot on our tail?"

"Uh, no?"

He laughed and brushed his hands together. "We'll need to make two trips."

Kate looked around the densely forested area. They were in Nowhereville, Tennessee, off some road that hadn't been repaved since before she was born. After leaving the grocery store, Luke had pulled the Blazer off the road and driven into the trees a good mile to get to the hidden three-wheeler.

He secured the groceries onto the back of the vehicle with bungee cords, then threw one leg over the seat and straddled the machine. "Hop on," he said with a grin, patting the seat behind him.

Kate eyed the ATV. "You're sure I can't drive?"

"No, you can't drive. Now hop on and hold on."

"What about Rembrandt?" She held the sleeping kitten up and Luke scowled.

"Give me the cat." He held his hands out.

Kate swiveled away, pulling the kitten out of Luke's reach. "What are you going to do?"

He sighed and wiggled his fingers in a give-me motion. "You can't hold on to me while you're holding that fur ball. Give him here."

She eyed him with suspicion. "And how are you going to do that and drive?"

"Damn it, Kate, do you have to argue about everything?"

"Yes."

He sighed. Reluctantly she handed Rembrandt over. The kitten's eyes popped open when Luke took it and it hissed. Luke muttered something under his breath, but he held it gently while he undid the top buttons of his shirt and slid the kitten inside. He winced and Kate imagined Rembrandt using his claws to gain his balance. She climbed on the three-wheeler and wrapped her arms around Luke's stomach, using her hands to cup the kitten inside his shirt.

The vehicle started up on the first try and Luke accelerated. Trees whipped by. Kate closed her eyes and buried her forehead against Luke's back. Forget about the murder charge, not to mention grand theft auto, she was going to die in some Tennessee backwoods, the victim of a three-wheeler gone berserk. Maybe Luke had been right in not letting her drive. This was scary, dodging in and out of trees. If they were following a path, she couldn't see it. Then again, she couldn't see much with her eyes sealed shut.

Twenty minutes into the three-wheel roller-coaster ride, Luke slowed and Kate felt comfortable enough to open her eyes. The trees had thinned. Before them, and tied to a dock, sat a houseboat, complete with water slide and Sea-Dos, bobbing on the water of a clear lagoon. The three-wheeler came to a stop and Luke hopped off, dug inside his shirt and pulled out a hissing Rembrandt.

"Here." He shoved the cat at her with another scowl while Kate climbed off, her gaze sweeping across the water.

"This is beautiful."

"Wait until you see the lake."

"I could stay here forever and not have to see the lake."

Luke laughed and untied the groceries. "You won't say that once you see the lake. Here's a key to the houseboat." He handed her the keys the clerk at the store had given him. "Take the groceries in and put them away while I go back for the rest. It'll take me a while since I have to take care of the Blazer. Pick whichever room you want."

"Is this yours?"

Luke hopped back on the three-wheeler. "Yup. Make yourself at home." He started up the vehicle and raced back into the line of trees leaving Kate alone for the first time in days.

Uneasiness crept along her spine as she glanced around the silent forest. Even though she'd lived by herself for the past eighteen months and had come to enjoy her solitude, she didn't like the feeling of being completely by herself now. *Don't be stupid, Katherine. He'll be back.*

With that thought, she grabbed a bag of food in one hand, held the kitten in the other and marched to the boat.

Houseboat was a loose term. This was more like a floating mansion with white siding and black tinted windows that wrapped all the way around. She found what appeared to be the entrance and tried the key in the lock. When the door swung open, cold air hit her in the face and that seemed strange. Wouldn't the place have been closed up? Did someone know they were coming? But those thoughts quickly fled when she stepped inside.

"Wow."

Her feet sank into a creamy Berber carpet. The walls had been painted a light tan and a caramel-colored leather sofa sat against one wall. Windows looked out over the lagoon while matching leather chairs finished off the cozy grouping. Beyond the living room, she caught a glimpse of the kitchen-slash-eating area with pine cabinets and full-sized appliances.

Kate kicked the door shut and sat the groceries and Rembrandt down. Her curiosity piqued, she meandered through the living area. The artwork of Seurat and Van Gogh hung on the walls and a vivid memory hit, stealing her air. She and Luke had known each other a few weeks and were strolling through the Cincinnati Art Museum, holding hands, whispering to each other in the hushed silence.

She'd visited the place often, comparing her art to the masters, in awe of their great talent. But this time was different. This time she had Luke with her and she felt light-headed with a feeling she'd never experienced before. Luke hadn't known a thing about art—true art—and she'd taken it upon herself to educate him, introducing him to her favorites. Seurat and Van Gogh. Did he remember that day as sharply as she did? Or did he simply like their styles and that's why he'd hung them on his walls? The paintings on Luke's walls weren't originals, but excellent reproductions.

Breaking the ties that bound her to the pictures, she stepped back and turned away, poking her head down the long hall, trying to shake the memories of a time when she'd felt carefree. Happy. Three closed doors were on the right, another wall of windows on the left. She opened the first door. A king-size bed sat on a high pedestal, facing an entertainment center complete with a large screen television.

Her step faltered as her gaze locked on the lone painting hanging over the bed. It wasn't one of the masters, but one of hers. Again her feet took her closer as her mind rebelled. She reached out, touched the roughened brush strokes with the tips of her fingers. She'd named this one *Contentment*. The title and the subject matter had nothing in common. It was a garden-variety still life—flowers and fruit set before a window. No, the title came from her frame of mind at the time she'd painted it.

The last time she'd ever been content. Luke had been living with her then. He'd taken some vacation time and had lounged around the house for a solid week. She'd been in the middle of this painting and he'd wander in while she'd paint, settle into a chair and read a book or just watch her create. He'd always said he loved to watch her draw and paint.

Soon after, he'd disappeared. It'd been one of the last pieces she'd completed. Unable to bear looking at the painting, she'd sold it to a gallery in New York along with several other original works.

She tilted her head, remembering now. Her agent had called a few weeks after Kate had given it to the gallery and in an excited voice, told her the astronomical price an anonymous buyer had paid for the piece. Kate had been relieved it was gone and happy it'd fetched a good price. Never in a million years would she have thought Luke was the anonymous buyer.

Absently, still deep into her thoughts, she climbed the steps to the upper deck. Festive, multi-colored rope lights were strung across the fiberglass awning. A bar with a stainless steel refrigerator and gas grill stood at one end, tables and chairs were scattered about the other. Kate propped her elbows on the railing and looked out over the calm water.

That old familiar longing returned. The need—wish—to be the person she'd been eighteen months ago, before her life turned in a deadly direction. Melancholy stole over her and she tried to shake it loose but it wouldn't budge. She loved the atmosphere of the posh houseboat, but the silence was almost too much. She didn't want to be alone anymore with her thoughts.

As she made her way back to the lower level, the late afternoon humidity settled on her like a wet blanket. Finding a lounge chair, she sank into it with a weary sigh.

The view would have made an amazing painting, and her fingers itched to recreate it as her mind went to the sketchpad and pencils Luke had bought her. But just as quickly as the urge came, she pushed it away and curled her errant fingers into her palms. It was all in her mind, this inability to paint. Everyone said so. But that didn't make a bit of difference. She supposed it was punishment, being able to look at something and see the beauty of it, yet unable to recreate it. Her own living hell.

The familiar weight of depression pressed in on her. She couldn't succumb now. Couldn't afford to go there again. Not when she'd just barely escaped it the last time.

From inside, Rembrandt mewled. Kate rose, let the cat out and resumed her position on the lounge. "What now, baby kitty?" Rembrandt pushed his head against Kate's hand and purred as she scratched behind his ear. "Where do we go from here?"

She stared out over the lagoon, at the thick stand of trees on the other side. Far off a fish jumped, creating rings that grew wider and wider, marring the perfection of the water. Funny how life was like that, one ripple bumping into another until a wave formed, slapping at the shore. If she hadn't gone into the gallery that fateful day nearly three years ago, she would have never met Luke or fallen in love with him. If she'd never met him, he would have never left her. And if he'd never left her, Laura would be alive today. Kate tipped her head back and blew out a sigh. Her family had told her to quit with the 'what ifs' but it was hard sometimes.

A car door slammed, making her jump. A few moments later something scraped against the fiberglass edge of the boat. Her heart picked up speed and her hand shook. Her stomach clenched in dread.

Luke wouldn't have brought the SUV back here. That had definitely been a car door. Suddenly her isolation pressed in on her and the hair on the back of her neck rose. She stood and turned around.

A stranger wearing a khaki sheriff's uniform, one hip cocked, the other knee bent, leaned against the opposite railing. Her gaze snagged on the shiny star on his chest. Her lungs inflated but refused to release the captured air. Then it all came out in a rush.

His lips pursed and he whistled low. "I do believe you're Katherine McAuley."

Kate shivered and wiped sweaty palms on her shorts as her gaze darted around the boat, searching for an escape. Surrounded on three sides by water, and the cop blocking her only escape to land, she had nowhere to go but overboard. Her floating palace had become a floating prison. She licked dry lips. Her mind screamed at her to run, to jump into the water, but that was blind panic talking and she attempted to swallow it, along with the lump lodged in her throat.

Damn it, she and Luke hadn't left a man to die in her living room, stolen a car, raced across two states and evaded capture only to have it all come down to bad luck and a nosy backwater sheriff. Luke's wit and courage had gotten them this far, certainly she could do her fair share.

Besides, they were only dead if they were *both* caught. She eyed the sheriff who stared at her. Could she get him out of here before Luke returned?

She took a step forward on legs that threatened to buckle. "Yes. I'm Katherine McAuley and I killed Lucas Barone."

Chapter Eight

The sheriff's eyes narrowed, and his lips puckered in a grimace. He tapped his hat on his thigh.

"You may as well take me in," Kate said, taking another step closer, surprised her voice didn't crack. "I confess. I killed Lucas Barone. Shot him in my living room. The jerk showed up on my doorstep after walking out on me." She tried to infuse all of the anger she'd felt toward Luke into her words. After all, they were words she'd thought a million times with far more malice than she said them now. She took another step forward.

The high whine of the three-wheeler broke through the peaceful chirping of the birds and the buzz of the cicadas. Kate tensed and the sheriff froze.

A few moments of silence followed as she and the sheriff faced off. She wanted to cry in frustration. She'd been so close. Another ten minutes and she'd have been gone. Now it was all over and if Luke's theory was correct, Suzanne would find them and kill them. As much as she'd wished it in the past, Kate didn't want to die. Not now. She closed her eyes as a shudder passed through her.

"Kate?" Luke called from inside.

She looked at the sheriff, whose head was cocked to the side, and he was staring at her in amusement. "I knew he couldn't be dead." His voice sounded husky with what could only be relief.

Luke burst through the door and stopped short, his gaze darting between the two. "John," he said on a released breath.

The man named John smiled. "Good to see you alive and well, Barone."

Luke looked at Kate, the relief evident on his face. She couldn't relax as easily. Her heart still thundered and her knees still threatened to buckle.

"I see you two have met." Luke indicated Kate with a tip of his chin.

"We met," John said. "Figured you'd show up here sooner or later, that's why I readied the boat. Didn't figure you'd bring your killer with you." The humor left his face. "What's going on, Barone?"

Luke indicated the glass-topped table surrounded by chairs. "You better sit down. It's a long story."

The three of them sat. Luke reached over to grasp Kate's hand and John's gaze followed the motion, then flickered to Luke. A silent message passed between them, something male that she couldn't decipher. At the moment she didn't care because she was afraid if Luke let go, she'd float away. Nothing seemed real anymore. Nothing made sense.

Luke filled John in on what had happened over the last several days. John listened intently, rubbing his scarred hand with his good one. Occasionally his eyes would narrow, but he remained silent until Luke finished. Then he leaned back in his chair and whistled low.

"Suzanne. Huh."

"You know her?" Kate asked.

"Oh, yeah. I know her."

"John and I used to work together at IATT until John

retired." From the tone of Luke's voice, Kate got the impression there was no love lost between John and Suzanne. Every time her name was mentioned, John rubbed his scarred hand harder.

John crossed an ankle over his knee and studied Luke. "So what now?"

Luke shrugged and adjusted Kate's hand on his thigh. The warm skin under the denim and the strength of his hand around hers brought her comfort and security.

"Right now, Kate and I are going to lay low for a few days. I need to look into some things but I can do that from here."

John nodded, pushed his chair back and rose. "Call me if you need anything. What'd you do with the Blazer?"

Kate jerked at the mention of the stolen car and Luke squeezed her hand. "They've discovered it's missing?"

"From the Cincinnati International Airport. You got here in the nick of time, my friend."

Luke looked off toward the lake, his expression grim. "The Blazer's well hidden for the moment."

John nodded again. His blue gaze flickered to Kate.

Kate stood, holding her hand out to him. "It was nice to meet you."

He looked at her hand and hesitated before reaching out and shaking it briefly, then letting go.

The men walked off, their voices low. From the back, they were two gorgeous males—John broader and huskier, Luke sleeker and more graceful. Both were deadly. And both were wounded. Both carried their physical scars on the outside, but they had equally brutal scars on the inside. Their eyes told the story.

But even without the haunted looks, Kate would know that.

Her own scars were buried deep but she recognized a kindred spirit when she saw one. She knew how she got her own scars, but what about John and Luke? What had happened to them? Was this what the government produced? Men willing to fight for the freedom of their country at the expense of their souls?

John stopped next to his cruiser and adjusted the brim of his campaign hat. Looking over the lagoon, his eyes had that faraway look to them, the one Luke remembered well.

When Kate had offered her hand to his friend, Luke held his breath. John didn't like to touch people, especially women, but he'd shaken Kate's hand. Only Luke knew what the action had cost his friend.

John opened the car door and leaned his elbows on it. "So what are you really going to do?" he asked.

"Like I said. I'm going to lay low." His gaze drifted to the houseboat and his stomach clenched. If he'd ever envisioned reuniting with Kate—and he had to be honest, he had—this wasn't at all how he'd planned it—enforced isolation and on the run from a deadly threat he didn't know how to counter. By every right, she should hate him, yet she'd gone along with everything, using her own quirky sense of humor to cope. "I figure I'll let the media frenzy over Kate die down, then confront Suzanne."

"How?"

He shrugged. "I don't know. I don't even know why she's after me. When I find that out, I'll figure the rest out."

"Take care of her." For the first time in a long time John's voice held something other than hatred.

"Who? Suzanne?"

"Hell no. Kate. She was willing to give up her freedom for you. She wanted me to arrest her."

"What?" Luke's gaze snapped back to John.

"She confessed to killing you. Wanted me to arrest her. Was pretty insistent about it, too."

"Like hell."

Chuckling, John threw his hat on the passenger seat of the cruiser. "Like hell nothing, buddy. She was willing to face a murder charge for you." He hitched his leg and climbed in. "If that ain't love, I don't know what is."

"Love?" Luke snorted. Kate didn't love him. He'd killed that emotion off a long time ago.

As John drove way, Luke stood alone on the patch of grass between the lake and forest, thumbs tucked into his pockets. Could John be right? Could Kate still love him? No. He refused to hope. Refused to believe. Refused to go there again. He told himself that as the hope blossomed and the belief took hold. Deep down, he knew he'd go there again. As long as Kate was with him.

He walked back to the houseboat and stopped short when he rounded the corner. She stood in profile, looking out over the lagoon, the setting sun bathing her in warm yellows and pinks. A slight breeze blew a few strands of hair around her temple while the cat lay on its back, batting her shoelace. The tanned length of her leg and the flash of her belly-button ring brought his body to sharp, almost-painful arousal. She was like no one he'd ever met before. Funny, talented, with a penchant to argue that at times drove him insane.

Before Kate, he'd dated sedate women who wore designer dresses, spoke several languages, talked with authority about stock portfolios and could plan a dinner party in under two days. After Kate, that sort of woman didn't appeal to him anymore. He'd suddenly found himself wanting a partner who talked football stats, had paint stains on her clothes and shopped at discount stores. One who wrestled with her brothers and somewhat calmly accepted that her ex-boyfriend shot a man in her living room.

He loved her. Had from the first moment he saw her.

She turned and smiled at him and the smile pulled him across the distance—years or feet, he didn't know. He just knew he needed to stand next to her, feel her heat, look at her.

Be with her.

She had known he was there before he even approached her. Had felt his gaze on her as she pretended to look out over the water. But when she turned to face him, she was unprepared for the tenderness on his face. Or for the weariness in his eyes.

She'd been so busy fighting her own fear over the last several days, being angry at him for dragging her into this and dealing with her rising feelings, that she hadn't given much thought to the toll this was taking on him. She saw it fully now and her heart went out to him.

He bent and leaned his elbows on the rail beside her, his gaze centering on the lagoon, the slight breeze brushing through his dark hair. Rembrandt hissed and took off to hide under a chair.

"So you used to work with John?"

He nodded but didn't say any more. She didn't get the feeling he was angry at her, just sad.

"Why did you want him to arrest you?" He'd yet to look at her and she took his cue by looking at the water too.

"Because you told me that if we were caught, Suzanne

would find us and kill us. I figured if just one of us was caught, the other would remain free to figure this out."

He didn't say anything to that, just kept looking straight ahead, his hands clasped in front of him. He was in a strange mood, one she'd never seen him in before, and she didn't know how to react to it. What she really wanted to do was reach over and hug him. Pull him into her arms and hang on tight.

"I won't let you turn yourself in." His voice was husky as if he were fighting back tears. "Don't you see? It'd kill me to see you behind bars for something I did. I brought you into this and I'll make sure you get out of it. But you *won't* be arrested. Understand?"

She was beginning to. "Out of a sense of guilt? Obligation?" She knew all about guilt. Lived with it on a daily basis. Sometimes it was all she could do to get through her day with the burden of guilt she carried on her shoulders.

"Yes. But it's more complicated than that."

She wanted to ask how much more complicated, but he surprised her by straightening and taking her in his arms. The warm, musky scent of him surrounded her and she wrapped her arms around his waist and leaned her cheek against his chest. "Oh, Luke." *Don't do this to yourself.* She wouldn't wish her type of guilt on anyone. Especially Luke.

His hand skimmed up her back, sending goose bumps and arrows of desire skittering down her spine to tingle in her toes. His other arm wrapped around her waist, anchoring her to him. She stared into gray eyes as stormy as the day was calm.

"Promise me you'll do this my way," he said, feathering his thumb on the sensitive skin under her jaw. She fought the tremor overtaking her insides. Fought the desire to lean in and kiss him. "Promise that we'll work together to get this solved." His eyes darkened even more and she bit her lip. "Stop arguing for once, Katherine, and promise. I know I lost your trust long ago, but trust me to get us out of this."

"I trust you."

His gaze searched her face, sliding over her chin and lips and cheeks until finally settling on her eyes. "Do you?"

"Yes."

He opened his mouth to say more, then closed it on a sigh. The look in his eyes told her he was going to kiss her, but she was still unprepared for the light touch of his lips, for the zing of need racing through her and for her desperate desire to keep him just where he was.

His tongue probed and hers answered. He pressed his hips into her, his arousal pushing against her. Her body responded by becoming wet, hot, heavy. She couldn't hold back the moan any more than she could stop herself from pushing against him.

Luke hissed in a breath, pulled away from their kiss and rested his forehead on hers.

Kate gulped mouthfuls of air trying to stop her mind from spinning out of control. She didn't need this. Look what happened every time he showed up. Her world was never the same again. No, she didn't need Lucas Barone. But she sure wanted him.

Later that evening, Luke occupied his hands by preparing dinner. Too bad he couldn't occupy his mind with mundane tasks as well. Unfortunately, or fortunately, depending on how he looked at it, he couldn't stop thinking about kissing Kate. Holding her in his arms. Feeling the smoothness and warmth of her skin against his palm.

The knife slipped and sliced his thumb. He yelped and stuck the bleeding appendage in his mouth.

Kate looked up from pouring tall glasses of iced tea. "You okay?"

No. "Cut myself," he said around a throbbing thumb that echoed a very different throbbing part. He turned back to cutting the stir-fry vegetables, ignoring the pain in his thumb and his shorts.

Dinner was strained, tense. Luke shot quick glances at Kate, only to find her staring at him, then turning away, a blush creeping up her neck. For a moment out on the deck, he'd thought they'd reached some sort of truce but he realized now that nothing would ever be easy with Kate. She'd retreated back into herself and he fought his growing frustration at the withdrawal.

Luke took a gulp of tea, the ice cubes clattering in the empty glass. He set it down and wiped his mouth with his napkin. "So tell me what you've been up to, Kate? What have you been doing since I...left?" As soon as her eyes darkened, he wanted to groan at the stupid question. All he'd wanted to do was make small talk to try to reconnect with her and the first thing to come out of his mouth hurt her.

But he'd wondered. For eighteen months, and most especially the three months in prison, he'd wondered what she'd been doing. Had she missed him or moved on? He'd wanted her to miss him but knew that was selfish. Yet, he didn't have it in him to hope she'd moved on. "How's your family?" he asked in an effort to divert her pain.

It seemed to work because her shoulders relaxed. "Fine."

"Your brothers?" He'd always envied Kate's brothers the camaraderie and the sense of family they'd had together. He'd never had that with his sister. Eric, Paul and Riley had accepted Luke as one of them but he didn't hold out any hope they still did, not after he left Kate the way he had.

A small smile lifted the corners of her mouth and a tenderness entered her eyes. "They're doing well." She paused as the smile slowly slipped away. "Except for Eric. He lost... Um..." She licked her lips, swallowed, dropped her gaze to the tablecloth. "L-Laura."

Eric's wife had been like a sister to Kate and Luke wondered if Laura's death was the added sadness he'd sensed in her. "I'm sorry. Was it sudden?"

She nodded but wouldn't look at him and he decided another change in subject was in order, but Kate beat him to it. "I saw my painting in your bedroom."

He stilled as he reached for his water glass, then dropped his hand to his lap, watching her closely. When he'd brought up her art before, she'd closed him off quickly. That she brought it up now, on her own, surprised him. "And?"

She traced a pattern in the tablecloth with her thumbnail, still not looking at him. "And I assume you're the anonymous buyer who paid a fortune for it."

"I am." On a rare visit to New York City, after his escape from Peru, he'd seen it hanging in the gallery. It'd hurt that she'd put it up for sale because it reminded him of happier times. Unlike Kate, he hadn't been able to let it go, so he'd purchased it, preferring to remain anonymous because he'd never had any intention of letting her know where he was.

"Tell me about your painting," he said. "What are you working on?" He studied her closely as his mind went to the empty guest bedroom in her home that had once housed her easel and paintings, to the pencils and sketchpad he'd bought that had so far sat unused.

She stiffened. "I don't paint anymore."

Luke sat back, his earlier nervousness gone. He was in his element now, a master at retrieving information. And he was determined to find out exactly what had happened to her dreams. "Oh?"

"I, um." Her gaze lifted to his then skittered away. "I'm a bartender."

It took him a moment to stop reeling from that bombshell and to absorb the implications. "You're a painter, Kate. You draw beautiful, emotionally charged pictures, not drafts." Anger rolled through him at the thought of her dodging the wandering hands of drunks. She was a painter, damn it. A great painter. Well on her way to becoming famous.

She stood suddenly, gathering her plate and his, avoiding his glare. "I'll clean up since you cooked."

"Tell me why you're not painting."

Pain flickered through her eyes right before she closed them. An answering pain twisted him into knots. Just what had happened to her? His leaving wouldn't cause the pain he'd seen in her. Something else, something terrible had happened and he needed to know because he wanted to help.

"I, um... It wasn't paying the bills."

"You're lying."

Her eyes flew open and she pursed her lips, anger darkening her expression. For a second Luke didn't know if she intended to throw her plate at him or take it to the sink.

"You have no right," she said, her voice wavering. "You left. And you didn't come back. You have no right to question my decisions, how I live my life."

"I can't pretend not to see your pain, just like you can't pretend not to see mine. What happened?"

Tears welled in her eyes, overflowed and dripped. "Damn you!" She put the plate down and swiped at her cheeks. "I don't paint anymore! Is that what you want to hear? I'm a bartender. I pour drinks and listen to people's pathetic stories. Or at least I did. I'm sure I'm out of a job by now." Her shoulders shook and the plate she was still holding trembled. "Just when I finally get my life back on track, you come falling through my front door and tear my world apart again!"

She slammed the plate on the table, whirled around and ran out, closing the door so hard the boat rocked. Luke stared at the dirty dinner dishes, at the overturned saltshaker and the empty iced tea glasses.

With shaking hands, he picked up his plate and took it to the sink. She had her secrets. He had his. Yet, he couldn't force her to tell him her secrets when he refused to divulge his. What a pair they made. Haunted, hurting.

Hunted.

He looked out the window over the sink, staring into the dark night, not seeing anything but his own reflection in the glass. He didn't like what he saw. He scrubbed a hand down his face but the action didn't erase the man he was.

Kate stood on the dock, staring into the dark recesses of the forest. The breeze whistled through the branches, the leaves rustled in the trees, the lake lapped against the side of the boat and the crickets chirped.

She shouldn't have said those things, even if they were the truth. Luke couldn't help it that someone was after him and she was glad he'd been there the night Hank Stuben broke into her house. Of course, Hank Stuben wouldn't have broken into her house if it hadn't been for Luke.

She took a deep breath of the still-stifling night air. She

should go back and apologize. The look on Luke's face right before she'd turned around and left indicated her words had cut deep.

But she couldn't go in. Because she was afraid. Afraid he'd bring up her painting. Afraid of his questions. Afraid of her answers. Afraid to divulge the awful truth of what she'd done. Afraid he'd hate her if he knew.

She stepped off the dock, her feet landing on hard, firm ground, and turned to look at the houseboat. Lights shone from the windows. Up top, the string of party lights created a festive rainbow, beckoning her to return from the dark night.

Luke's form floated past the kitchen window. The lights backlit him until he was nothing but a dark shadow against bright yellow.

She could have sworn their gazes touched, but that was impossible. She couldn't really see him and he probably couldn't see her. A breeze brushed past her and she shivered, clutching her arms about her waist and rubbing her elbows.

She felt more alone out here, looking inside Luke's houseboat, than she ever had in her entire life. In the past, she'd always had her family to turn to. She and her brothers fought like cats and dogs, but when one needed the other, they were always there.

Now every time she returned home, she thought she saw the condemnation in her family's faces. The accusations.

She looked away, toward the black void of the lake.

"Kate?" Her head snapped back to the boat. Luke stood on the other side of the dock. "Come back inside, Kate." His voice was disembodied, husky, beckoning, calling, inviting. She shivered again. "I promise I won't ask any more questions about your art." Now his voice held defeat and sorrow.

Kate took a hesitant step toward him, then another and

another until they stood inches apart. Silently he held out his hand and she grabbed onto it.

Together they walked back into the light.

Chapter Nine

Kate woke to bright sunlight pouring into her room, Rembrandt curled up on her chest and the crisp smell of bacon and pancakes. She stretched, causing the kitten to tumble off her and land on the bed.

Her stomach rumbled and she threw the covers off, pawed through her small supply of clothes and dressed in a pair of running shorts and a t-shirt. Scraping a hand through her hair, she made a quick trip to the bathroom before stumbling into the kitchen where she froze in mid-yawn.

Luke stood at the stove, flipping pancakes onto a plate, dressed in swim trunks that reached his knees and a short sleeve shirt unbuttoned over a tanned chest. A baseball cap sat on his head, the brim turned backwards, sunglasses perched on top. A day's growth of beard darkened his cheeks and jaws. Her mouth watered, but not from the aroma of buttermilk pancakes. What did her in were his bare feet. He looked so at home, so comfortable, so unlike the Luke she'd known for the past several days.

He smiled at her, and it made her tingle. She'd buried those memories of lazy mornings with him, talking about everyday things, small things, but this morning brought them all back. And this time the memories didn't hurt. They were warm and inviting and comforting like the food Luke was cooking.

"Hungry?" he asked.

"Oh yeah."

He shot her a confused glance and she cleared her throat and headed for the breakfast bar that separated the living room from the kitchen. She was hungry all right. Hungry for the past, for the easy cadence of the life they had created together. Hungry for normality and yes, hungry for him.

"This place is amazing," she said, indicating the houseboat—anything to take her mind off what she couldn't have.

"Thanks." He flipped another pancake on a plate and slid it in her direction.

She reached for the butter and syrup. "When did you buy it?"

He paused in pouring a cup of coffee as if he had to weigh his answer. "About a year ago."

Kate cut her pancakes with the side of her fork and paused before shoveling it in her mouth. A year ago? She'd pictured Luke going on with his life. But the fact he lived a normal, everyday existence still startled her. It even hurt a little. Yet what good was her hurt? They'd gone their separate ways and that was that. She put her forkful of pancakes in her mouth and chewed. "Mmmm. Good."

His gaze met hers and hot desire flared in his eyes, then disappeared when he blinked. "Glad you like them."

"So what's the plan for today?"

Luke shrugged, leaning against the counter and concentrating on his breakfast. "A little boating. A little swimming."

"No investigating? No trying to track down Suzanne?"

He scraped the last bit of pancake into his mouth and

shook his head. "No need to track her down. I know where she is."

"Really?"

He nodded.

She'd thought she'd be relieved to get this whole thing over with, but now she realized that meant she and Luke would part ways. While that was what she'd wanted a few days ago, this morning she wasn't so sure. Since last night on the dock, she and Luke had reached a tenuous peace. And she didn't want to give that up just yet.

He turned to the sink and rinsed off his plate. "But that doesn't mean anything. I have to figure out what's going on before I can contact her."

Kate pushed her empty plate away. "Why don't you just ask her?"

"Because she wants me to figure this out for myself. She likes cat-and-mouse games. Especially when she's the cat."

Luke stacked the dishes in the dishwasher and wiped the counters down while Kate sipped her coffee. He glanced at her while he continued to wipe. "I, uh, have a satellite phone if you want to call your family. It's untraceable."

She went still. "You'd let me do that?" She'd been wondering what her parents were going through since the media released the story about her. They hadn't been pleased with Luke after he'd taken off, but she didn't think they'd believe she killed him. Yet she'd wanted to talk to them, to at least tell them she was all right.

He'd squeezed the dishrag so hard that soap bubbles dripped through his fingers and onto the counter. He wiped the soap off on his swim trunks. "Of course I'd let you call them." After he finished straightening the kitchen, he motioned for her to follow him into his office. Pulling open a desk drawer, he

109

extracted a small phone with a long, thick antenna and dialed a series of numbers.

"This will scramble the call in case the police put a trace on your parents' phone. Just dial their number the way you normally would." He handed her the phone.

Kate's hands shook as she dialed and Luke let himself out, closing the door behind him as the phone on the other end began to ring.

"Hello?"

"Mama?"

A long pause followed while Kate held her breath. "Katherine?" Her mother's voice came out soft and breathless. "Katie, is that you?"

"It's me, Mama." She shoved a fist against her mouth to stifle the sob building in her lungs. She pictured Sandra McAuley sitting at the kitchen table, her hair perfectly combed in the chin-length bob she preferred, dressed in faded jeans and a t-shirt, her usual at-home attire.

"Are you okay, baby?"

"I'm fine. I wanted—" She swallowed, forcing away the lump in her throat. "I just wanted to let you know I'm okay." Her mother sobbed. Tears rolled down Kate's cheeks and fell to the polished mahogany desk. "I'm sorry, Mom."

"What happened, Kate? They say you killed Luke."

"I didn't. I swear."

"Katherine Anne McAuley! Don't you think I know that? Where are you, baby girl? Are you hungry? Cold?"

Kate closed her eyes on the overwhelming pain. "N-no. I'm fine," she whispered. "I'm safe and I'm well-fed and warm. Please don't worry about me." She brushed the tears away, but new ones took their place.

"Katherine?" Her father's gruff voice made her jump.

"Daddy?"

"Where are you, girl? Your brothers and I are ready to come get you. We'll fix this mess you've gotten yourself into."

Her brothers were there? Eric, too?

"Are you okay, sweetheart?"

"I'm fine, Daddy."

"You tell us where you are, Katie-girl." His voice held that stern tone that made her spill the beans every time. "I swear, Katherine Anne, if you don't tell me, when I get my hands on you..."

She swallowed a smile at the all-too-familiar words. He was trying so hard to hide his fear behind a gruff exterior. "I'm fine, Daddy. Really."

"Hold on," he said in resignation, "someone wants to talk to you."

"Kate?"

Her shoulders drooped as her stomach tightened into knots. Eric.

"What the hell's going on, Katie?" He sounded angry and her body trembled. Silence hummed along the airwaves.

"Katie, talk to me." His voice switched to a low, sweet tone. The voice of her favorite brother. The one she'd sent into a spiral of grief because of one wrong turn. She closed her eyes. "I'm here to help you, sis. Don't freeze on me now. Tell me where you are. I want to help."

Her tears came faster now. All the grief. All the pain. "I'm sorry, Eric." And she didn't mean for the predicament she was in.

His sigh was heavy. "We've been through this before. Now's not the time to go over it again. Tell me where you are and I'll come get you. I promise. We'll get you out of this."

Almost the exact same words Luke had spoken to her yesterday.

"It's too complicated to explain right now." She knew his mind was working overtime, reading between her words, looking for a chink in her armor. Riley and Paul used their brawn to intimidate. Eric used his brains. And in her case that worked far better than muscle. "I'm sorry you had to come home for this." Since the accident, Eric didn't visit often. He'd closeted himself away with his grief and his work as a U.S. Marshal.

"Turn yourself in. Running isn't the answer, Katie. Face this problem with the truth. You didn't kill Lucas Barone, we know that. Tell me where you are. I'll come get you. Together we'll go to the police."

She shot a guilty glance at the closed door.

I know I lost your trust long ago, but trust me to get you out of this.

"Kate, let me help you. I know people. You wouldn't have to spend any time in jail. We'll post your bond right away. You can come home to Mom and Dad."

...trust me to get you out of this...

Her mind raced over the events of the last several days. Luke grabbing her hand and racing with her out of her house. He could just as easily have left her to face the police alone. Luke caring for her while she suffered through a migraine. He could have, and probably should have, kept going instead of stopping at a motel for her to sleep it off. He'd endured her arguments and her anger. He'd helped her through the paralyzing shock after they'd run from her home. She pictured those haunted, hunted gray eyes that stared at her with sadness.

"Kate?"

"I can't, Eric."

"Damn it, don't be obstinate now! Let me come get you. Just tell me where you are." His voice went from angry to cajoling.

"No," she whispered into the phone.

"You're being ridiculous."

...trust me...

"No. I'm keeping safe. T-tell Mom and Dad I l-love them, and I'll see them soon." She disconnected. Leaning her elbows on the desk, she covered her face with her hands as tears fell down her cheeks and sobs shook her body, until she became nauseated.

"Are you okay?"

Beside her, Luke crouched down on his heels and she slithered off the chair and into his arms.

Luke wasn't above eavesdropping, not when it came to their safety. He'd heard her end of the conversation and knew her parents had used Eric to try to get her to turn herself in. He'd stood on the other side of the door, breath held, waiting for her to capitulate and reveal their location. He'd known the risk in letting her call home. But he also knew Kate and the torture she must have been going through wondering how her parents were holding up. It was a risk he'd been willing to take. But to his complete surprise, she'd refused to divulge their whereabouts.

"You better get me out of this like you promised, Barone."

Her words were like splinters wedged under his skin. Now that she'd placed her trust in him, he felt the weight of the world settle on his shoulders. Could he do it? Could he get them out of this? And if he did, how would it change them?

He settled on the floor and gathered Kate onto his lap, hugging her to him and stroking her hair while he muttered words of solace, words he couldn't even recall once they left his lips. His bare chest was wet with her tears, but he didn't move, couldn't move. Her grief nailed him to the floor.

He'd make Suzanne Carmichael pay for this. He'd meet her at the doors of hell if he had to, but she'd regret the day she framed Kate for his murder. He placed a tender kiss on top of Kate's head. No. Hell didn't scare Suzanne Carmichael. Only one thing frightened that woman and he'd use that fear to his advantage.

He'd use the media against her. Reveal to the American people the viper she really was. When he got through with her, she'd be stripped of her political power. And she'd be nothing.

Kate turned another page in the book she was doing an admirable job of pretending to read. The apple she was eating tasted like sawdust and felt like sand in her mouth.

All because of Luke, who lay on the chaise mere feet from her, asleep. The sun beat down on him, but that didn't bother his slumber. One tanned, muscled leg lay on the chair while the other was bent at the knee, his foot firmly planted on the deck. Barefoot again. Geez, she had a thing for his bare feet.

His hands lay loosely folded on a stomach that revealed every ridge and hollow. His scars were a dull white against his bronzed skin, the bruises now dark blue and purple. Every time she glimpsed them, she got a little jolt. A reminder that the man who lay before her wasn't the same man she had fallen in love with.

She turned another page and took another bite of the

tasteless apple. The words on the page blurred, much like they had for the past hour. Aggravated and hot, she threw the book down.

"You okay?" Luke asked without moving.

She drummed her fingers on the arm of the chair. "No."

Luke pushed himself up and crossed his ankles, looking wildly disheveled and not the least bit hot. "Are you thinking of your parents?"

She shook her head. Surprisingly, her family hadn't entered her mind after she'd emptied her well of tears all over Luke. The decision had been made. She'd cast the die in Luke's direction and was comfortable with her choice.

She rose from the chair and prowled the deck. "Why aren't you doing anything?" She threw her hands up in frustration.

Luke raised an eyebrow from behind his dark glasses. "What would you have me do?"

"I don't know. You're the G-man, you tell me."

He shrugged. "You're right. I should be doing something. But I want to enjoy the day, Kate. It's beautiful, the lake's beautiful." His gaze roamed her swimsuit-clad body. "You're beautiful."

Her skin heated, and this time it had nothing to do with the humidity or the pounding sun.

"Enjoy the reprieve," he said.

She paced to the railing and looked down into the lake. After breakfast, Luke had cast off from the dock and piloted the boat into Catawba Lake. She spied fish, dozens of feet below, swishing their fins, oblivious to the heat and turmoil above.

"I can't." *Yes, you can. Just let yourself go. Let yourself enjoy.* But she was afraid to enjoy, afraid to let down her guard. What if Luke found his way into her heart and broke it all over

115

again? What if he discovered her secrets? *Face it, Katherine Anne. Luke never left your heart. He's still there. When he leaves this time, he'll break your heart all over again.* She sighed as the truth of that sank in.

She searched for something to take her mind off Luke. "Tell me about John Callahan." She turned just in time to see him tense.

"You want to know about his scars."

Her gaze skittered to his own scars and she nodded. "That and how you know him."

He looked toward the hills rising up from the lake, his lips thinning into a tight line. The muscles in his upper arms were rock hard, his breathing fast.

The silence dragged on, broken only by the lapping of the water against the hull and the occasional cry of a bird. "You're not going to tell me, are you?"

"We worked together."

"Did you get your scars on the same mission?"

"Yes." He bit the word out, almost as if it'd been pulled from him against his will.

She sank into the nearest chair. "What happened?"

"I can't tell you. There are things I can never tell you, Kate. My security clearance won't allow it."

She had a feeling his own inner demons wouldn't allow it either. "It must have been bad."

His laugh was brittle, forced between bloodless lips. Despite the heat of the day, goose bumps rose on his arms, making the fine hairs on them stand up.

"How long ago did this happen?"

A host of emotions crossed his face—despair, regret, anger, acceptance. She swallowed past her dry throat. Her heart beat so hard she could actually feel the pulse in her neck. She waited, forcing herself to breathe.

"Eighteen months ago."

Her hands twisted in her lap. "Is that why you left?"

Again silence fell. This time not even the birds chirped. Luke looked toward the trees on the shore, but she would have bet her life savings he didn't see them. "I had no choice." His voice was faint, as if he spoke from a long distance.

He swallowed. She wanted to reach out and touch him, offer what support she could, but his body language forbade it.

"Why didn't you call me, tell me?" She'd left to go to the gallery, and when she'd returned, he was gone. How many times had she lain awake at night wondering if he was alive or if it was something she'd done to make him leave? To learn it hadn't been her merely raised more questions. If not her, then what? Why?

"You don't know how many times I wished I'd called you. If only to tell you I loved you one more time."

"Why didn't you?"

A long pause followed as if he had to organize his thoughts, pick the right words, put them in the right order. "I didn't expect to meet you when I first came to Cincinnati, but there you were. And there I was. And suddenly I was feeling things that...scared me."

Her bottom lip trembled as memories escaped her tight hold. So many good ones. Long walks through Eden Park, longer talks while sitting on a park bench eating ice cream cones, holding hands, waking in the morning with their arms and legs wrapped around each other. Hot nights, hotter lovemaking. They were all there, all rushing back.

Luke pulled his gaze from the tree line, his expression

tormented.

"Tell me the truth. Why you were in Cincinnati when we met?"

His lips thinned and he seemed to think about his answer. "Do you remember the Mosque bombing? It made the national news. People thought it was a terrorist plot so I was sent down to check it out. Turns out it was nothing but a hate crime. Serious, but not serious on the IATT scale." He shrugged. "The rest you know. I was walking through the downtown area, came across the gallery with your paintings and stopped in."

She'd always thought it was fate that she'd stopped in the gallery at the same time to check on the progress of her next show. They'd met then, attracted to each other, drawn together by her art.

The attraction hadn't dimmed or fizzled, but grew stronger. Luke had told her he was a forensic accountant working for the government, deciphering accounts of criminals, the mob, terrorists. An innocuous job, he'd said, but his own contribution to the war on terror. And she'd believed him. She'd believed him every time he'd been called away, every time he'd stayed away for weeks.

Eventually he'd moved in with her, giving up his residence in Chicago.

"I couldn't handle my feelings for you," he was saying. "And I couldn't reconcile my life as an operative with my life with you. They were two separate things. One good. One not so good. It wasn't until I was gone, and I knew I couldn't come back, that I realized just how much I loved you."

"Why didn't you call then?" she asked.

The shadows that crossed his face made her want to recoil. "I wasn't the same man anymore." He laughed and it was a bitter sound. "Hell, I wasn't even human anymore."

"What happened?"

"Everything."

"Tell me."

He ran a shaking hand down his face and rubbed his cheek. Suddenly he stood and walked away, entering the houseboat. The door closed with a quiet click, leaving Kate alone.

She stared at the closed door for long moments, unable to follow him for fear of what she'd learn. Her head already reeled with his admissions. He'd been scared of them, of his feelings for her. And had carried around a tremendous amount of guilt over the lies he'd been forced to live. She didn't quite know how to deal with that let alone face what else happened to him.

She listened to the cicadas and birds, the low drone of a motor boat that wandered close to their position. Sweat dripped down her back, but inside she shivered. She'd learned a lot, yet nothing.

The door opened and Luke strode through, an opened beer bottle in one hand and a glass of iced tea in another. He handed her the tea and resumed his seat in the lounge.

"I got a call that one of our operatives had been taken by The People of Light. They needed my help in getting him out." He spoke as if there'd never been an interruption in the conversation.

Kate took a sip of the tea, sweetened exactly as she liked it. "Was it John who had been taken?"

"Yes." He took a swig of his beer and began pulling off the label, his head bent. "I went down there to see what I could do." His hands shook as he shredded tiny pieces of foil. Kate held her glass in both hands, the ice cooling her. "His captors refused to talk to me. I had word from a source within the prison that John wouldn't last through the night so I offered to make a switch. John for me."

Kate clutched the glass harder. Her breath lay suspended in her lungs. She wanted him to stop talking. She wanted to plug her ears. Torture. He was talking about torture. John near death. Him taking John's place. That meant he'd been tortured too.

Suddenly it began to make sense. The cries in the middle of the night in Spanish. *No mas* meant *no more.* Had he been begging them to stop? Her stomach clenched and she wrapped an arm around it to keep herself from bending over in horror. The scars. All those scars...

"They took me up on it."

The glass in her hand slipped, but she managed to hold on to it. What did it take to make a decision so heroic you knew it would likely end in your death? A very horrible death. Could she have done that? Laura's laughing face flashed before her eyes. If she had known beforehand, would she have switched places with Laura?

"Don't look at me like that."

She blinked. "Like what?"

His lips curled in a snarl. "Like I'm some damn hero," he growled. "I'm not."

To her he was, but now wasn't the time to tell him that. "H-How long were you in prison?"

"Three months."

Oh, God. The apple and her tea threatened to come back up. She forced the nausea away with a will she didn't know she possessed. Three months. "How'd you do it? How'd you survive?"

He drank the last of his beer, his throat working to swallow it. Sweat beaded on his forehead and rolled down his chest.

"Who said I survived?"

Chapter Ten

Luke leaned forward and clutched the kitchen countertop. He dropped his head and took deep breaths. His forearms and biceps shook, his legs barely holding his weight.

Since his debriefing, he'd never, ever spoken of that time in Peru. At first the nightmares had consumed him until, like a baby, he'd begun to fear the coming night. For a long time he'd slept with the light on. The smallest noises made him jump. It'd taken months to return to a semblance of the man he used to be, and he still wasn't the same person. His captors had taken a vital part of him and crushed it.

But not all of him. Not the part that had hoarded his memories of Kate.

He raised his head and took several deep breaths, his eyes shut tight. Right now the memories were strong, overpowering, but they would fade. They always did. Just as they always returned. He needed to get drunk, to drown the images flickering in his mind, but he couldn't do that. Even though Suzanne didn't know where he was, that didn't mean they were safe. Protect Kate. That was his goal. He worked better with a goal, with a plan. A purpose. Protect Kate.

A warm hand touched his arm. He flinched and recoiled, too lost in his memories to differentiate Kate's touch from his captors. He whirled around and Kate took a hurried step back.

"Not now, Kate." He forced the words from between clenched jaws. He couldn't even see straight right now, let alone form a coherent sentence.

Her gaze, full of sympathy, flickered over his face.

That was the last thing he needed or wanted. To hell with people's pity. He'd made his decision in that South American jungle. Only *he* could offer himself pity. She reached for him again and he took a step back.

"There's a boat approaching."

He stilled, his nightmares taking a back seat to a new fear. "What?"

She waved her hand toward the lake at his back. "A boat's approaching. I thought they'd turn away, but they just keep coming."

With Kate hot on his heels, Luke strode into his bedroom and grabbed his Glock. Standing to the side of the window, he motioned for Kate to do the same before peeking between the blinds. He should call John for backup, but the boat was too close.

He released the magazine on his weapon, checked the ammunition and slammed it back into place. Pulling the slide back to chamber a round, he turned on his heel. And ran smack into Kate, who lost her footing and stumbled back. He grabbed her upper arm, leaned down and kissed her, pressing his lips against hers with a bruising force, needing to sear the feel of her into his brain just in case this was the last time.

He pulled away and stepped around her, leaving her standing in the middle of the room with a blank look on her face. "Stay here," he commanded, and shut the door behind him.

He carefully made his way through the kitchen, instinctively keeping to the shadows. A familiar coldness overtook him. His eyesight honed to razor sharpness; his hearing intensified. He made his way to the stern, hoping to God Suzanne was on that boat because he was in a mood to tear her apart. One day. One lousy day he'd been given with Kate.

As he pulled open the door, the sun blinded him and he pulled his sunglasses over his eyes. A speedboat sat not thirty yards off starboard.

Kate stepped up behind him, keeping to the shadows of the interior.

He growled in frustration. "Stay back. Don't let them see you."

A man, burnt red from the sun, stepped onto the bow of the speedboat. Luke tightened his grip on the Glock, keeping it down low against his outer thigh. The man swayed, a bottle of beer in one hand, the other raised in greeting. Another man piloted the boat while a third lay sprawled in a seat, apparently passed out. "Hellooooo," the man called out. His foot slipped and he windmilled his arms to get his balance.

"Beautiful," Kate murmured.

"Keep your eyes on the other two," he said, keeping his voice low and trying not to move his lips.

"I don't think that one's going anywhere anytime soon."

With his free hand, Luke waved to the drunk teetering on the bow, forcing a cheeriness to his voice. "What can I do for you?"

"Saw the boat. Wondered if you needed help."

They had drifted close enough that Luke could see the drunk eye his boat. "No problems," he called back.

The man nodded while the driver slid his sunglasses down his nose and looked the boat over, his gaze zeroing in on Luke, eyes narrowing. In suspicion? Recognition? He couldn't tell with the damn sun in his eyes.

"Thanks for the concern though," he yelled across the water.

The sunburnt man looked disappointed. "You sure?"

Luke nodded and waved. "See ya 'round."

The driver said something to the man on the bow. The drunk shot him one last look—startled? Or was Luke reading too much into this—nodded and climbed down, slipping and sliding across the fiberglass. The speedboat's engines rumbled to life when the driver hit the throttle and the boat's bow rose. They turned and sped off, leaving a wake that rocked the houseboat.

Only when they were nothing but a white dot on the far side of the lake did he turn.

"Well, that was interesting," Kate said, stepping out of the shadows.

Luke grunted in agreement. "Keep out of sight for a while. I need to call John, see if he knows anything about these yahoos."

He stood at the window in his office and dialed John's cell. When the sheriff answered, Luke relayed the description of the boat and the numbers on the side.

"Yeah, I know of 'em," John said on a sigh. "They come up once a year, cause trouble, then go home. I wouldn't worry about them."

After he disconnected, Luke continued to visually search the lake. He felt marginally better knowing the boaters weren't sent by Suzanne, but the episode reminded him that he wasn't here for fun and sun. Damn it, Kate didn't deserve any of this. Somehow he would clear her name and confront Suzanne, but for the time being he wanted to enjoy Kate's presence. He wanted to make love to her, sleep with her cradled in his arms and wake with her in the morning. He didn't know how much time they had left, but he planned on milking every last second.

With one last long look at the horizon, he turned on his heel, and headed back to the front of the boat where Kate lay on a chaise in the shade. "You know what?"

She looked up at him with a startled expression. "What?"

"We need a little fun around here." Tossing his weapon and sunglasses on the nearest table, he scooped Kate up and threw her over his shoulder. She shrieked and grabbed onto his waist. He grinned and slapped her bottom.

"Lucas Barone, put me down! What are you doing?"

He climbed the spiral staircase, careful not to bang her head against the wall.

"Lucas!" She giggled. When was the last time he'd heard her laugh? The night before he left. She'd been happy then. Carefree. He hadn't seen her like that since. Truth be told, he hadn't laughed much since then, either. He crossed through the party deck, heading for the slide attached to the upper portion of the boat.

Kate pounded his back, gasping with laughter. "Luke. Please."

He set her on the slide and pushed. She slipped away, a blur of blue suit and flailing legs and then went airborne. Her yell was cut off when she hit the water and Luke laughed until tears formed in his eyes. Kate surfaced, then went back under, her arms slapping the water.

She bobbed back up. "Can't...swim." She sank again.

Luke stopped laughing and straightened. He quickly climbed up the slide and pushed off, opting for safety because he didn't know how deep the lake actually was at this point. Kate bobbed up one more time before the lake swallowed her. It was like a bad B-movie, her hand waving until even her fingers disappeared under the waves. Luke hit the water and dove under. The lake was clear and he had a good view of Kate struggling. He grabbed her under the arms and hauled her up.

She broke the surface with a gasp. Luke gulped in air, his heart beating hard against his ribs. "God, Kate. I'm sorry. Are you okay?"

She giggled, wriggled free and performed a perfect dive beneath the surface. She pushed away from him, her body all sleek muscle, tanned skin and blue suit. Hair slicked back, eyelashes glittering with drops of water, she surfaced once again, laughing. Incredulous, he could do nothing but tread water and stare at her. She'd *tricked* him!

She wiped the water from her face and grinned, her blue eyes dancing with amusement. "Swim team all through high school."

"You..." Luke didn't finish the sentence. He dove after her and found himself laughing at her antics. This was the Kate he'd fallen in love with. This was the Kate who'd pulled him through three months of imprisonment.

Her laughter drifted to him from above the water line. Her legs kicked out and she shot away from him, her thigh muscles bunching and flexing with each stroke. He managed to grab onto her toe, but she slid free. Bubbles rose to the surface as he chased her.

She lay on a bright green raft they'd pulled off the boat, the sun's rays drying her. Luke propped his elbows on the raft, his legs making lazy circles in the water. She grinned. His dark hair, all slicked back from his face, appeared black. Little squint lines radiated from the corners of his eyes. It made her happy to have erased the bitter pain she'd witnessed earlier. *Who said I survived?* He'd survived, whether he wanted to believe it or not, and she planned on proving it to him. Somehow.

"I didn't know you were on the swim team."

"Seems we're even then. There're things I never knew about you either."

He winced and she reached out, smoothing the frown lines from his forehead. "I didn't mean it that way. I meant it as fact."

"Are you angry I lied to you?"

"I was."

"I'm sorry," he said.

"Apology accepted." After he'd told his story about Peru, she'd realized it was time to move on, time to discard the old hurts. Actually saying the words lifted a weight from her chest. She sighed and looked up at the cloudless sky. "Let's forget about Suzanne and just stay here forever."

"You wouldn't want that, Kate. Eventually you'll want to go out in the real world. And we need to clear your name."

"I suppose you're right." But at the moment, Suzanne Carmichael, murder charges and dead men named Hank Stuben seemed far away.

Luke leaned up and pressed his lips against hers. They were cold and wet, yet her mouth went dry and her body hot. She slid off the raft and into his embrace. For the first time she wished he'd bought her a two-piece bathing suit so she could feel his skin against hers.

Luke wrapped his arms around her while they tread water

to keep from sinking. Their thighs brushed against each other, the fine hairs on his legs sending electric currents through her. As he pressed an open-mouth kiss to her neck, she shivered, and tipped her head back to give him easier access. He sighed, running his tongue from her ear to her collarbone. The heat gathering at the apex of her thighs became a throbbing need. Her hip brushed against his erection and he gasped, nipping her earlobe.

"I want you, Kate."

Their tongues met and danced. Luke's hands cupped the back of her head, balling her hair into his fists and they sank, never breaking contact. Luke's powerful legs kicked and they both rose to the surface. He grabbed the raft in one hand and Kate's hand in the other. They made it to the swim platform somehow and Luke pulled himself up, his biceps flexing with the effort. He reached down and lifted her out of the water. Together they hurried to his room.

Luke's bed sat on a high pedestal, requiring a stool to get up. Luke climbed it and knelt on the bed, his swim trunks dripping, and Kate quickly followed, kneeling in front of him. His fingertips glided down her arm, barely touching, causing a shiver to start at her toes and work its way up.

"You don't know how much I've missed you." He pushed her wet hair from her face so she could see him better.

"Oh, Luke. I've missed you, too." She touched his cheek, brushed at a drop of water clinging to his strong jaw. A part of her didn't believe he was here, about to make love to her. Her eyes burned with unshed tears as so many emotions backed up inside her. For so long she'd pretended to hate him, even blamed him for what had happened after he left. Now she realized her hate was nothing but her defense against the aching grief he had left her with.

His blue gaze flickered over her face, stopped at her eyes. "I would take it all back if I could," he whispered.

She shook her head, shushed him by pressing her finger against his lips. As much as she would like to believe him, as much as she thought he believed it, she knew it wasn't true. "I understand," she said. "John needed you and I wouldn't want you to abandon John."

"I should have told you..."

She shook her head again. "For once let's leave the past in the past. Make love to me, Luke."

He tumbled them onto the bed and tugged the straps of her swimsuit down, revealing breasts puckered from the cold and the need to be touched. He stared at them until Kate nearly whimpered in frustration.

His gaze rose to meet hers. "Is this real?" he asked. "I can't help but think I'm still in prison and dreaming of you."

"I'm real. This is real."

With a low growl, he dipped his head, his tongue snaking out to lightly touch a protruding nipple. Kate threw her head back, a groan coming from between parted lips. His hand played with the other nipple, rolling it between his fingers. She arched her back, pressing closer to him, this time silently begging. He turned his head, scraping his five o'clock shadow gently across both nipples.

His arm came around her back and he climbed on top of her, his head dipping down once again. This time he took her entire nipple in his mouth and sucked with greedy abandon. Kate gasped and grabbed fistfuls of his hair, anchoring his head to her breasts.

Her hips bucked against his erection, searching, searching. Her stomach clenched. Luke's tongue laved her, not letting up on the pressure. The room spun, her mind swam.

130

Luke lifted his head and skimmed his hands down her sides to her hips, her outer thighs. He peeled the bathing suit the rest of the way off. She couldn't move to help him, could barely breathe.

"You—" He kissed her. "Are—" Another kiss. "So beautiful."

Her head lolled to the side as she whimpered, her body responding yet again to his mouth.

"Please, Luke."

"Don't you worry, angel. I'll take good care of you." He parted her thighs with his knee, his cold, wet skin sticking to her. His eyes had gone dark, his pupils dilated. His nostrils flared right before he leaned in and took her mouth in a possessive kiss. He plunged inside her and she winced, her body stretched to its limit, burning with the intrusion.

He stopped and stared down at her. "Look at me, Kate. Look at me so I know I'm not dreaming."

She stared up at him. "I'm right here, Luke. Feel me?" She lifted her hips and he groaned. "Right here with you." She wrapped her arms around his neck, pulled him closer. "Always," she whispered.

He closed his eyes and cursed softly. "I'm not protected, Kate. Are you?"

"What?" She fought through the decadent fog of her brain. Protected? Oh! *Protected.* "No."

He pulled out and she whimpered again. He'd reduced her to nothing more than whimpers and groans. The warmth of his body disappeared and, chilled, Kate shivered. Somewhere far off a drawer opened, cardboard ripped, foil crinkled. Then he was back, sheathed for her protection, and this time he slid in easily.

Eyes tightly closed, lips thin, lines of concentration etched in his forehead, Luke thrust forward. His movements were slow, even, and they drove her over the edge. She wanted fast and hot. She pressed her pelvis into his and grabbed his tight rear end, urging him faster, harder, stronger. *More.* His eyes opened, almost black as night.

"Easy, Kate. Slow."

He kept up the maddening pace. Another orgasm began to build and her eyes widened in surprise. His self-assured smirk met her gaze.

"I can't survive another one."

He took both her hands and raised them above her head. "Yes, you can."

She shook her head, not able to form the words.

"Yes. You can."

The lines of concentration around his eyes became strained, but still he kept it slow. Maddening. Frustrating. She was on the edge, teetering. Her muscles clenched. Luke gasped. His hips rocked. She arched into him, his name bursting from her lips, ending on a groan.

He pumped into her, driving himself as far as he could. Her orgasm flared to life again, milking the entire hard length of him, shattering her into millions of particles of light and sensation. He arched his back, the muscles in his neck and shoulders straining. Their cries mingled, as they shouted each other's names together.

Chapter Eleven

Luke settled down beside Kate. Her muscles may have turned to jelly and her bones may have melted, but despite that, Kate rolled with him, not wanting to lose his warmth or the skin-to-skin contact. He threw an arm over his eyes as she stacked her fists on his chest and rested her chin on them.

"Did I wear you out?"

He shot her a one-eyed glare from under his arm, then lifted his arm and settled it over her back, running his fingers up her side. His hand floated up and played with a curl dangling on her shoulder. "This is how I survived."

She stilled, her grin fading. "What?"

"Earlier you asked me how I survived." His gaze locked on the curl in his hand. "When it got too bad, I thought of you."

"Luke, don't..." *Don't what? Don't shatter the moment? Don't tell me because I'm too much of a coward to want to hear what you've been through?* She didn't know. She just wanted to stop his flow of words, to go back to a place where they'd been happy. Her gaze scanned the scars and bruises on his torso as she tried to shut off the horrid images of how he got them. Luke beaten. Luke hungry, cold, thirsty. *Hurt.* "The things I thought when you left—"

He put a finger to her lips and her gaze collided with his. His eyes were a deep, stormy gray, his suffering apparent in the

133

swirling depths. "You had every right to your thoughts."

She shook her head, dislodging the tears that had been building. Not those thoughts. He'd been kidnapped and tortured, while she'd been safe in her own home, railing at him for leaving her, hating him for giving up on them. But he hadn't abandoned her. Hadn't turned his back on her. He'd *remembered*. She closed her eyes as the tears continued to flow. How could she ever be worthy of his love?

"Ah, Katie." He wiped a tear from her cheek. "I didn't tell you to make you sad. I told you so you'd know I've never forgotten what you mean to me."

Suddenly she was glad he'd never told her what he did for a living. Because when he disappeared, she would have *known*. Those awful images now racing through her mind would have been a constant loop she wouldn't have been able to withstand. Ever since he'd returned, she'd wondered what had happened to change him so much. Now she had her answer. And it scared her.

Because she wasn't the woman he thought she was. She wasn't strong. After he left, she'd done things. Things he wouldn't be proud of. Things *she* wasn't proud of. She wasn't the same person he fell in love with and that made her want to cry all over again. For lost love. For lost time. For loss.

"You're pulling away, Katie. Please don't do this."

"It's just...I'm not strong."

He brought her in for a swift hug. "Yes, you are. No other woman could have handled the last several days with the humor you have."

She shook her head. "You don't understand. When you left, I changed. I'm not the same person anymore."

He held her face between his hands and looked at her. "Its okay, Kate. I'm not either."

A tear dripped down her cheek, off her chin and landed on his chest. She studied the drop of glistening wetness. When she moved to scoot away, he pulled her in tighter.

"You aren't leaving me," he whispered against her hair. "I won't allow it."

Luke didn't want to remember those months after his release, but for Kate he'd do it. To keep her from pulling away. To make her understand when he didn't even really understand himself. His thoughts, his reasons were muddled, but one thing he knew for sure was he needed to come clean, to explain. And in his cleansing he hoped Kate would take his lead and cleanse her own guilt from her tortured soul.

He threw an arm over his eyes and consciously willed his mind back to that time.

"After I got back, I spent a lot of time in and out of hospitals. But that was just the physical stuff. The mental took longer." Images swirled in his mind, terror, loneliness and desperation, pain and confusion. And that had been after he'd been rescued. "John kept telling me about this lake nestled in the mountains of Tennessee. So I came here, bought the houseboat. I needed...to be alone for a while." He reached out and ran his fingers down her arm, tracing the line of goose bumps that had popped up. John had been a strong force, all but ordering Luke to survive when he'd wanted to do nothing but crawl in a hole and die. "I went back to work. But inside I was... I couldn't seem to feel." And he refused to go back to her like that.

But now Kate had managed to storm the barrier and glimpsed the abyss that ate at what was left of his soul. And when she didn't turn away, the darkness had turned to light. For the first time, he pushed the memories of that horrific time into a room and closed the door. They would never completely disappear, but at least now they wouldn't haunt him.

"So what changed? Why suddenly show up on my doorstep now?" she asked.

"You mean besides being beaten?" His grin was fleeting. She'd asked him that before, in the car, and he'd managed to evade answering. But there were no more evasions. "I've asked myself that same question, and the only answer I come up with is that it was time."

She seemed to think about that for a long time before he felt her nod. "Yes," she said quietly. "Maybe you're right. Maybe it is time." She climbed on top of him, her thighs straddling his hips, and leaned down, her breasts brushing his chests. "No more."

His hands settled on her hips. "No more what?"

"No more hiding behind barriers. No more refusing to feel. No more secrets."

Ah, the pot calling the kettle black. He pushed a hair out of her face. "Only if you do the same." His fingers drew lazy circles on her hips.

Her eyes widened to a brilliant blue and dilated with desire. Or was it panic? "What do you mean if I do the same?" She shifted, putting more of her weight on his erection. A driving, pulsing need took hold of him. The lazy exploration of his fingers became more deliberate, more searching.

"You've been hiding behind your own barriers, Kate. And you've been keeping your own secrets."

"Oh yeah?" She bent and licked his nipple.

Tingles shot up his spine and he gasped. She was trying to distract him, but that was okay. For now he'd let her. Pleasure took over the need to speak. A driving force that eclipsed all thought. Words became moans while breaths mingled. Together they soared, hands held, souls searching for a healing touch. And in the aftermath of their lovemaking, Luke couldn't help but hope they'd moved closer together. That they'd begun to learn of the new people they'd become.

As his heart returned to a normal rhythm, he picked up the thread of their abandoned conversation. "The goofy way you were dressed when I first saw you. What was up with the jewelry and weird clothes?"

Indignation replaced the sultry, satisfied look he'd put there. "Goofy? Weird? I'll have you know, all that jewelry was handmade as well as the clothes. I was merely supporting the local art community."

"Uh-huh."

"And as for weird. That was nothing." She waved a hand in the air and Luke was reminded of the first time he'd seen her after falling through her door. She had changed once again. It went deeper than the missing bracelets and purple nail polish. There was a maturity to her. A depth that came from descending into hell and coming out on the other side. He'd seen it in himself. He'd seen it in John. And now he saw it in Kate.

"You should have seen me with black hair," she said.

"Black?"

"Uh-huh. With a pink stripe."

"Pink?"

"Well, not always. Sometimes it was yellow and sometimes green."

"Green." He felt a little green around the gills himself thinking of Kate with black hair and a green stripe. What had her ultraconservative parents said about that new and different

Kate?

"Yup. Green. It took forever to get my hair back to blonde. In fact, if you had shown up a few weeks earlier, you wouldn't have recognized me."

"Really?" He leaned up and kissed the underside of her jaw.

"Really."

Hours after the euphoria of their lovemaking went from a boil to a simmer, Kate quietly slipped out of bed, pulled on one of Luke's shirts and made her way to the upper deck where she leaned against the railing and let the humid breeze clear her mind. What had she been thinking making love to him again? He was good, honorable, decent. And she was not.

Because she wasn't just running from a murder charge—she was a murderer.

Resting her elbows on the railing, she propped her chin on her fists.

Warm hands slid around her waist as Luke urged her back against his bare chest and rested his chin on the top of her head. "It's a beautiful evening," he said.

She nodded, her gaze locked on the clear water before them, her stomach twisting into knots. What she would give to turn back the clock.

"Missed you in bed."

Luke had spilled his painful secrets and she could do no less. She only hoped he'd still want her after he knew.

He rubbed his chin against her hair. "Deep thoughts?"

"Yeah."

"Care to share?"

Not really. But she had to. "I killed someone." Kate held her breath, waiting for his withdrawal.

Instead, he merely held her tighter. "I'm assuming we're not talking about Stuben."

"No." She paused to gather her courage. "After you left, I went to D.C. to visit Eric and Laura. They were expecting their first baby." All the memories she'd tried to hold at bay came crashing back, making it hard to talk around the lump in her throat.

Luke kissed the top of her head. "Go on."

"And...I...I needed to get away. I was so hurt."

"Ah, Kate, I'm sorry. All I can do is apologize." After a stretch of silence he spoke again. "So you went to D.C..."

"I went to D.C. and spent time with Eric and Laura. They were so happy, so looking forward to the b-baby." That morning, Laura had shown her pictures of the sonogram. She'd pointed out little toes and a femur. He was sucking his thumb. Kate had been awed. And saddened. Everything had made her sad then.

Luke shifted, bringing her back to the present and the awful reality of what happened.

"Laura and I went to lunch. She wanted to check on the crib she and Eric had ordered. I-it was a bright day, hot for April. The cherry blossoms were in full bloom." Funny how she remembered the cherry blossoms. Behind her, Luke was silent. What was he thinking? Did he know where this was headed? Was he already condemning her? "I was driving. Laura and I were talking." It was the first day after Luke had left that she actually started to feel like herself. And the last. She closed her eyes. Her body tensed and Luke rubbed her arms in a slow circular motion.

"I drove up the exit ramp." It was so clear in her mind, like she was right there, reliving it. She could even hear Laura's bright chatter. "I turned onto the main road." A tear slid from beneath her closed lids and landed on her hand. "Th-the car came out of nowhere. I swear I looked both ways." But had she? Had she really looked both ways? Ah, God, for so long she'd tried to remember and couldn't. "Suddenly the car was there...a-and I swerved because he was a-all over the road. Laura screamed." She shuddered and in her mind tires squealed, metal scraped against metal. "He hit the passenger side. Where Laura was." Horns from the oncoming cars blared. She fought to bite back her sobs. "She stopped screaming."

Luke's breathing came fast, his chest inflating against her back. The muscles beneath her hands were tense.

"Sh-she d-died." Kate sniffed and wiped her eyes, but the tears kept coming as she struggled with the next words. "Th-they...buried...Eric's son...in Laura's arms." The last word ended on a whisper followed by a sob that would have doubled her over had Luke not been holding her so tightly.

"Katie." Luke turned her and wrapped his arms around her. "It wasn't your fault, Kate." Luke tilted her face up until their gazes locked. "It wasn't your fault."

"I know."

"Do you?"

She shrugged and averted her gaze. The rational part of her mind believed it. But the emotional part, the part that had to look at her brother and see the grief still etched in the lines of his face, took all the blame. If she and Laura hadn't lingered in the restaurant after lunch. If they hadn't stopped in that bookstore on their way to the furniture store. If she'd looked to her left one more time before making that fateful turn...

"You can't change the past, Kate. It will always be there. It's

140

what you do with it that matters." She rubbed her nose and tried to pull away but Luke tightened his hold. "What does Eric say?"

"That I should let it go. That it wasn't my fault."

"And has he moved on as best he can?"

Eric had aged over the past few months, become withdrawn, quiet, overworked. But he'd picked up the pieces of his life the best he could. "Yes."

"Then why haven't you?"

She jerked back but couldn't break Luke's hold. "Because he wasn't driving the car. Because he didn't listen to his wife scream. B-because he wasn't *there*." Her words ended on a sob and she buried her face in Luke's chest once more. He rubbed her back and held her until she couldn't cry any more. But he didn't pull away. And that went a long way towards healing her soul.

"What would Laura want you to do?"

Kate thought about that for some time. "Laura would want me to kick your butt for leaving the way you did."

Luke laughed. "And after that?"

"She'd want me to live my life. Be happy."

"I'd say that's pretty good advice."

Kate looked up at him. "How do you do it, Luke? How do you live with the memories? The pain?"

"One day at a time, Kate. One day at a time."

Kate scratched behind Rembrandt's ears and listened to his low purr. An iced tea sat at her elbow, a beautiful lake lay in front of her and Luke lounged beside her, sipping a Scotch and watching the sun dip below the tree line. His head rested against the lounge chair, his eyes closed. The slight breeze brushed through his hair and a five o'clock shadow dusted his cheeks and chin.

She'd unburdened her soul and Luke hadn't walked out on her, hadn't docked the boat and told her to get lost. He'd been kind and concerned and loving. He'd listened when she'd talked, held her when she cried. And she was beginning to heal. The memories had retreated to a small place inside her, no longer taking up so much room. Now they allowed room for other things. Like hope.

Could she and Luke be happy together? A small tremor of apprehension shimmered through her. Now that she knew what he really did for a living, could she live with a man who up and left in the middle of the night headed for unknown destinations? Who constantly put his life in danger?

As if sensing her thoughts, he opened one eye and looked at her. "What are you thinking?"

"I—" Her hand dropped to her side and she swallowed the words. *I love you.* She wanted to say them, longed to say them, but the questions haunting her wouldn't allow it.

His other eye opened. "You what?"

"I think we need to talk about Suzanne."

The ice clinked in his glass as he raised it to take a sip, but his gaze never left hers. He seemed to dare her to say something else.

I love you. Rembrandt's cold nose butted her hand and she resumed scratching him. "Maybe if we go over that last night again, we'll discover why she's hunting you."

He took another sip.

"After the dinner you went home, right? And you were attacked inside your house."

"Correct."

"And everything was normal before the dinner?"

"As normal as my life gets." He looked out over the water, his voice flat, his expression shuttered.

"You don't want to talk about this, do you?"

He shrugged. "In order to get you back to your life, we need to figure this out."

Kate stood, plopped Rembrandt down on the chaise she'd just vacated and crawled up next to Luke. He scooted over to make room for her, draping his arm over her shoulder.

"Is that what you want? Me to return to my life?"

He sighed, jiggled the ice in his glass and looked at the water. She put her hand on the glass to stop his fidgeting and with her other hand turned his chin until those storm gray eyes looked at her. "Do you want me to return to my life?"

His jaw clenched, a muscle jumping under her hand. "What do you want me to say, Kate?"

She swallowed, her stomach twisting and a lump forming in her throat. The fingers caressing his chin trembled. "I want you to tell me where I stand in your life. Tell me where you see us headed."

He paused, shook his ice, then stopped. A frown creased his brow. "I see us headed in the same direction we were headed the last time and it scares the hell out of me."

"What scares you?"

"That my job will pull us apart again."

Tears pricked the backs of her eyelids but she forced them away. There'd been too many tears over the last few days. Over the last year and a half. It was time to move on, time to forgive and while she'd never forget, it was time to let go of the past. For both of them. "Know what I want?"

His lips quirked in a smile. "What do you want?"

"You."

His smile widened.

"As for your job, I don't have an answer to that. We'll just have to deal with it, I guess."

"What if... What if I quit my job?"

Her heart seemed to skip a beat. "What are you saying?"

One shoulder lifted in a shrug. "I don't know. Just that I've been thinking. I love you, Kate and...and I want a normal life."

The air left her lungs in a whoosh and she laid her head on his shoulder. Her body felt like melted wax that wanted to ooze all over him. "I love you, too."

He shifted her onto his lap, facing him, and planted a big, hard kiss on her lips. He smiled and rubbed noses with her. "You don't know how many times I've said that in my dreams."

She draped her arms over his shoulders. "Say it again."

"I love you. Now your turn."

"I love you, too."

"So what now?" Their noses still touched, his breath glided over her, smelling like rich Scotch.

"Now... Hmmm..." She had some ideas.

He slapped her bottom. "Not that. I have to get the boat back to the lagoon before night falls."

"Ah." She feigned disappointment.

"Ah hell," he leaned in and kissed her again, all hot breath and hotter hands sliding over her skin, under her shirt, cupping her breasts. "We've got a little bit of time."

✧

Suzanne ran a weary hand across the back of her neck and massaged the aching muscles. *Where are you, Lucas Barone? Where've you hidden yourself?* She tried to focus on the papers in front of her but was so tired the words blurred and she had to blink. There were a lot of crazy people in this world. She'd bet the Oval Office most of them had called the hotline with information on the whereabouts of Katherine McAuley.

For the third time, she rifled through the stack. She didn't trust anyone else to do this, to sift through the hundreds of phone calls of people who had supposed information on McAuley. Some kook in Cleveland claimed he knew Katherine intimately. That they'd been beamed up to a UFO together two years ago and had been implanted with tracking devices.

She only wished.

She shuffled through more papers, one outlandish report on top of another. Two men in Tennessee claimed to have seen Lucas—

She sat up straight, quickly scanning the report. They'd seen Lucas on a houseboat out on Catawba Lake. Lucas. Not Katherine.

She swiveled her chair to her home computer and tapped on the keys until a screen popped up. After the debacle in Peru, John Callahan had quit his job with the agency and disappeared off the radar. But not her radar. She'd kept track of him out of necessity, and remembered that he had retired to Catawba Lake.

When another screen popped up, she sat back. "Ah, Lucas. You've made a fatal error, my friend."

John Callahan lived in Catawba Lake, Tennessee. John Callahan. A ghost from the past or a mere coincidence? She didn't believe in coincidences.

Of course. She should have thought of it before and it angered her that she hadn't. Was she losing her touch, or just weary of the campaign trail and worrying about her fragile house of cards falling down around her?

She buried her head in her hands. Okay, if those two men recognized Luke, then they had to go. She didn't need the complication of any more bodies littering up her life, but she had no choice. She couldn't have them spouting off to the media that Lucas Barone was alive and well, living on a houseboat in Tennessee. No, that wouldn't do at all.

But she had him now, dead to center.

Lucas was hers.

Chapter Twelve

The bag crinkled as Kate pulled out a veggie chip. She aimed the remote control at the TV and surfed through the hundreds of channels the satellite provided. Thankfully her story of murder and love gone bad had given way to more pressing news. She didn't think she could watch any more of her life plastered across television screens all over America. But that didn't mean they were out of danger, as Luke continually warned her.

They'd spent the night in each other's arms, alternately making love and planning the future. When every sentence started with, "After this thing with Suzanne is cleared up," Luke got angry. He'd sat up in bed, running a hand through his tousled hair. "Damn it, we can't do anything until I figure out what Suzanne's up to and we get your name cleared."

"We'll figure it out."

He turned tormented eyes to her. "What if we don't? God, Kate, *what if we don't?*"

"We will." She pulled him down next to her and eventually they both slept. But when she woke this morning, she'd found Luke holed up in his office on his computer, trying to figure a way out of this mess.

She tossed the remote on the couch and rose, padding across the deep plush carpet to stop in the doorway and look in on him. A white polo shirt pulled tight across his shoulders, highlighting his tan. His hair stuck up in odd directions as if he'd run his hands through it numerous times. The light from the computer screen bathed his face in blue.

"Do you have anything other than veggie chips around here?"

"Regular chips are bad for you," he answered without looking up.

She rolled her eyes. "Are you hungry?"

He grunted.

She walked over to him, lifted his hands off the keyboard, scooted his chair back and plopped down on his lap.

He blinked at her. "What?"

"Have you found anything?"

His hands went to her hips as he leaned sideways to look at the computer screen. "No."

She leaned to the side to block his view. "I've been thinking."

"Positively scary."

"Very funny. I've been thinking about the night you were attacked."

His eyes finally focused on her. "Yeah?"

"You went to the dinner. Talked to Suzanne."

"Correct."

"You talked only to Suzanne and Bradley?"

He shrugged. "A few others."

"You said you went outside for fresh air?"

"Yes, but I came back in when I saw Brad talking to someone."

"Who was he talking to?"

"Hazim Zamal."

"Translate."

"Zamal is the Saudi foreign minister."

"And why would the Saudi foreign minister be there? I thought you said it was a small party."

Luke stilled, his fingers digging into her hips. "You're right." He laughed and smacked a big kiss on her lips, then pushed her off the chair and rolled closer to the keyboard. His hands flew across the keys.

Kate planted her hands on her hips. "Tell me what I said."

"I had assumed Zamal and Bradley were meeting for campaign purposes. But maybe I was wrong. After all, Zamal hadn't actually gone *in* to the party. Why would they meet outside?" He shook his head and laughed again, his eyes glued to the computer screen. "Great spy I am not to notice something like that."

"Why would you? You had no reason to suspect the Carmichaels of..." She frowned. "What do you suspect them of?"

"I have no idea. But something's up. I can feel it."

It was easier to believe him than question him. Besides, that gut feeling of his had saved her life several times. "Did you overhear what they said?"

"No. But I saw the body language. Brad wasn't happy and Zamal looked smug." He shook his head again. "I should have seen this before."

"I don't see why. You were beaten. Then there was that thing with Stuben, the stolen car. The race to get here."

He ran a hand up her thigh, stopping just short of her cutoffs, but he didn't take his eyes off the screen. "You're right. I was distracted, but that's no excuse. I should have known." His hands manipulated the keys. Screens popped up and disappeared, replaced by others. Several times a box appeared, demanding passwords and security clearances.

"Are you hungry?" It was well past one and he hadn't left the office since she'd gotten up that morning. "Luke?" He waved a hand in the air. Kate sighed, turned and left the room.

The rain had stopped and it looked as if the sun wanted to shine through the thick clouds. She went into her room and hung up the few clothes she had, humming as she threw the sheets over the bed. But when she reached for the comforter she paused.

Rembrandt wound his way around her ankles. Kate wiped her sweaty palms on her shorts and reached for the sketchpad and pencils lying on her bed, but stopped mid-way, fingers outstretched and reaching, wanting, needing. But old fears and old insecurities held her back and her arm dropped to her side.

She did an about-face and caught her reflection in the mirror above the dresser. She took a hesitant step closer, then another and another until she stood face-to-face with herself. She touched the cold glass, traced the outline of the curls corkscrewing around her face.

No neon pink streak. No green. No long hair to hide behind. No funny-looking clothes or jewelry to disguise the person inside. Nothing but her. Here she was, for all the world to see. And what exactly was she? She'd made a mistake and suffered the consequences. Wasn't that enough? Wasn't it time to move on?

If Luke could survive what he had, she certainly could as well.

She turned around and, before she could change her mind, snatched up the pad of paper and pencil and stalked into the living room. She stopped and looked around, her creative juices sluggish at first, then gaining speed until they raced through her. Settling on the leather couch, her legs tucked under her, she caressed the cool paper. It wasn't nearly as good as the sketchpads she had at home, but she didn't care. It was a blank sheet. And she could make it into anything she wanted.

At first her hand was unsteady, the lines wavy and crooked. Disgusted, she ripped the paper from the pad, balled it up and tried again. A few more attempts and it all came back. Smooth, sure strokes. Long lines, short feathery shapes, a smudge with the tip of her thumb to add shading and slowly Rembrandt appeared on the page.

She finished that drawing and went on to the next, but this one didn't come as easily. Discouraged, she drew back and looked at it with her artist's eye for details. She'd failed to catch the right emotion in the eyes. Frustrated, her creative energy at full tilt, she ripped the page off and tried something else. The smooth glass of the lake water. The hills rising above its surface. The reflection of the trees.

When she finally stopped and arched her aching back, the sun had almost descended and hours had passed. Hours she couldn't remember. She smiled in satisfaction and at the same time rubbed her throbbing hand. She'd done it! Just like Luke, she had conquered her fears and the devil within and had come out the winner.

Luke lifted his hands from the keyboard and rubbed his aching wrist. His back hurt from hunching over the keys. His eyes burned from staring at the screen and his head pounded from concentrating too long. He glanced out the window, surprised to see the moonlight filtering in, then at the plate of food Kate had fixed hours ago. He probably should eat, but he wanted to see Kate first. He stood and stretched his cramped legs and cocked his head. The houseboat was silent. She'd probably gone to bed.

Careful not to wake her, Luke left his office and made his way to the living room, passing through the kitchen. He had to smile at the evidence of Kate's attempt to get him to eat. Dirty dishes sat next to the sink. The faucet dripped. Crumbs lay on the counter, the opened loaf of bread sat next to a knife smeared with peanut butter. As he made his way through the living room, he bent and picked up crumpled paper. If they married, this was what life would be like. Picking up after Kate.

He didn't care. He'd gladly pick up after her if that meant having her forever. And he fully intended on having her forever. But first he needed to solve their current predicament.

And he'd finally had a breakthrough. He'd learned Bradley Carmichael owned stock in a major oil corporation along with Hazim Zamal. By breaking into computer systems from here to Saudi Arabia, Luke had tracked the profits from the corporation and compared it to the Carmichaels' bank accounts. There were discrepancies all over the place that raised red flags in Luke's mind. He felt good about his progress but uneasy about the next step he had to take.

He picked up a sheaf of papers lying on the coffee table and sat on the couch. He needed to call Callahan in the morning. He and Kate were out of time and they needed John's help. Luke absently shuffled the papers in his hand as he made plans for the next several days, but he paused when he caught sight of what he held.

He flipped through the papers again, a wide smile breaking across his face. She'd perfectly captured the haughty look on Rembrandt's face. Luke felt he could reach out to touch fur that looked so real he fully expected to feel it. He paused at the picture of himself. It wasn't the strong bold lines that stayed his hand, but the sadness. Did he always look like that? Had he let

Peru take over his life, or was it the absence of Kate that had lodged that look in his eyes?

He put the drawings down, suddenly needing to see Kate. But when he checked her room, she wasn't there. At some point she'd attempted to make the bed. The comforter was crooked, the pillows thrown haphazardly across it. Her clothes hung in the closet, but her shoes cluttered the floor.

She wasn't in his bed either. Then he spotted muted light coming from his bathroom and he peeked in. Lining the edge of the Jacuzzi were emergency candles propped in wine glasses that were filled with what looked like flour. Kate lay with her head against the edge of the tub. The humidity from the warm water made her hair curl around her face and had flushed her skin. Bubbles frothed up and over her chest.

His body hardened as his heart flip-flopped. He wanted her. But he wanted her in more than the physical sense. He wanted her mind and soul. He wanted her thoughts. He wanted to be inside her, around her, beside her. He wanted to wake up to her bright smile every morning and to fall asleep with her heartbeat next to him every night. He wanted it all.

He stepped back into the shadows of his room and shucked his clothes. She opened her eyes when his foot slid along her leg as he stepped in.

"Well, hello."

"Hi." He could barely speak through the tightness of his throat. The bubbles surged up and over the edge of the tub as he settled next to her. She climbed onto his lap, wrapping her soapy arms around his neck.

"Learn anything?"

He teased her nipple with his soap-slickened fingers. Her head fell back, her chest arching toward him. A long, low moan escaped her. Soft murmurs mixed with the scent of bubbles.

Whispers intermingled with the soft swish of water. An owl cried out in the night. The boat bumped against the dock. Hands skimmed wet skin. Lips glided over driving pulse points.

Luke placed his hands on her hips and lifted her up and over his erection. More water sloshed onto the floor. Silky skin skimmed against soapy skin. Kate rose and fell into a rhythm much like that of the waves on the lake—slow, easy, mesmerizing.

The pressure to empty himself inside her became unbearable and he gritted his teeth against it. Kate urged him on, whispering in his ear, nearly driving him past the point of no return. His control slipped, then slid away. The feel of Kate tight around him, her slickness, the scent of her, called to him like a pulsing drum beat, steady and sure, never wavering, never stopping. Her muscles grabbed at him and a low, keening cry ripped through the silent bathroom as she tensed in his arms, consumed by her orgasm.

His eyes flew open. Her breasts were mere inches from his lips, her head thrown back, ecstasy written across her face. "Kate?"

Her lids lifted, heavy and slumberous. "Hmmm?"

"I'm not wearing a condom."

She shrugged, eyes drifting shut, her hips moving him closer and closer to release.

He grit his teeth again, unable to pull away. Unwilling. He swallowed and the voice of reason intruded. He wanted nothing more than to plant his child in her, but not before their future was solid. His orgasm rushed at him, taking him by surprise in its intensity. The feel of Kate, just Kate and nothing more, drove him on. He didn't want it to end, but knew it had to. Head thrown back, the muscles in his neck straining, he cried out, and at the last minute, lifted Kate off to spill himself outside her. A sense of loss mixed with disappointment curled through him.

Kate's hand reached up and she stroked a finger down his cheek. "Someday," she said, her voice muffled because her lips were pressed to his shoulder blade. "Someday."

The next morning Kate sat at the breakfast bar and watched Luke fry up a dozen eggs and a pound of bacon. This from the man who thought potato chips were bad for him? With a distracted air, he scraped scrambled eggs onto a plate, heaping it high. Higher than she could possibly eat. He slid the plate toward her and added four pieces of bacon. Her heart seized just looking at all that cholesterol and fat.

She picked up her fork and shoveled some eggs in her mouth.

Just as Luke took his first bite, the outside door in the living area slammed open. Luke dropped his plate and grabbed for his gun. Kate slid off the stool and turned.

John stood in the doorway, dressed in a faded pair of jeans and an unbuttoned plaid shirt with the sleeves cut off. His hair was disheveled and a wild, hunted look shadowed his eyes.

Behind her Luke cursed and rounded the bar. "What happened?"

John's chest heaved in a deep breath. He seemed to gain some control over himself even as he ran a shaking hand through his ruffled hair. "Those yahoos on the boat the other day?"

The eggs Kate had just eaten threatened to come back up. She leaned against the bar, bracing herself.

"They're dead."

She squeezed her eyes closed.

"How?" Luke's voice was hard. When she glanced at him, his expression was even harder.

"Explosion," John said.

"Foul play?"

"Not as of now but we haven't had time to look. I just got the call and came here first. I've got to get over there."

"You think Suzanne did this?" Kate asked. How could Suzanne have known? Those men were drunk, looking for a good time. Harmless, she had thought.

Luke was all motion, moving to the stove and turning off the burner. "Get your stuff together," he bit out. "We're leaving."

This must be what he looked like while working. No emotion. No inflection in his voice. Every movement precise and clipped. Kate felt her own coldness begin to close in, to block the warm emotions she and Luke had finally managed to reveal.

"Now, Kate." He hadn't even looked at her since John had walked in.

"I want to know why you think this is Suzanne," she said, directing her question to both of them.

"Gut instinct." Luke dumped eggs and bacon in the trash, then tossed the plates in the sink.

Gut instinct. She'd trusted his instinct before and it'd saved her life. She didn't want to believe it now but had no choice. Without another word, she walked into her bedroom and threw her few clothes into a bag.

Chapter Thirteen

It didn't take long to clear out of the boathouse and get on the highway. Kate balked only when she realized she'd have to leave Rembrandt, but John assured her he would take care of the cat and close up the boathouse.

Luke drove John's borrowed pickup with a determination she'd never seen before, even the night they fled her house with Hank Stuben dead in her living room.

"Where are we going?" she finally asked.

"D.C."

Into the lion's den. A shiver raced up her spine and she rubbed the goose bumps on her arm. "Why?"

"Because it's time we went on the offensive. It's time we end this."

"You learned something last night, didn't you?"

He told her about his discoveries and his belief that Bradley was lining his pockets by driving up the price of oil.

"But that doesn't make sense," Kate said. "Why would Suzanne want you dead because of that?"

"Suzanne's driven, Kate. She wants to be in that White House more than she's wanted anything in her life. For Suzanne, it's about the power, and she's been aiming for this for a long while."

157

"So she feels threatened." She still didn't get it. Suzanne had power in the position she held now. "So what does this mean for us? Why go to D.C?"

"The Carmichaels are throwing a party. I need to be there. I need to get into their private computer."

"So hack in."

He shook his head. "I can't. The computer I'm thinking of isn't connected to the internet. There's no way in except to use it."

She'd trusted Luke with her life for the past several days; she'd trust that he knew what he was doing now. "Okay. What do we need to do?"

His lips tightened, the skin around them going white. "I need Eric's help."

Her heart fell to her stomach and her stomach dropped to her toes. Eric was the last person she wanted to talk to. But her personal issues couldn't matter now. "Okay. Hand me the phone."

Luke shook his head. "No. This is something I have to do."

"Barone, where the hell's my sister?"

Luke wasn't surprised Eric had figured out he wasn't dead and that Kate was with him. "Hello, McAuley, nice talking to you, too."

"Cut the crap. Where is she?"

"Safe."

Eric muttered an expletive that had something to do with parts of Luke's anatomy.

Luke clenched his jaw and ignored Eric's curses. "I need your help."

A long pause followed. "Reeeeally."

"Sarcasm doesn't fit you."

"Kidnapping doesn't fit you."

"Touché."

"What's going on? And I want a full report, Barone, before I agree to help."

He'd agree. His sister's life counted on it. But Luke gave him the story anyway, leaving out nothing except that he and Kate were back together. For the moment, that was between them. If and when the time came, he'd face her family and apologize, then ask for her hand in marriage. *If* they made it out. His gaze flicked to the rearview mirror, searching for a tail.

"So what do you want from me?" Eric asked.

"The Carmichaels are throwing a party tomorrow night. I need someone who can get in. Someone I can trust, who'll let me in the side window in the study where the computer's located. Then I need that person to keep an eye out, make sure I'm not discovered."

"I'm assuming that someone's me?"

"Yes."

"I'll do it. But only for Kate. As far as I'm concerned you can rot in the grave you're supposedly in right now. One invite?"

Luke glanced at Kate and hesitated. "Two. Kate's going with you."

Luke had to pull the phone from his ear as a long string of curses that questioned his parentage and called him every lowlife name in the book was thrown at him. Kate shot him a concerned look, her complexion a little paler than a few minutes ago. He didn't like the idea any better, but had no choice. There was no one he trusted now. His home had been broken into and he wasn't leaving her alone in a hotel room. It was either take her or leave her to the lions.

When the sputtering stopped, Luke spoke. "Suzanne found our hiding spot. Three men were killed. I can't leave Kate alone. If we doll her up, she won't look anything like the pictures on TV." He hoped. "Besides, what better place to hide her than right under Suzanne's nose?"

"You're insane."

There was that.

"And you're putting Kate's life in danger."

"Her life's in danger no matter what. I figure with you protecting her, it's in less danger."

Her brother paused, apparently out of arguments. "Fine."

After discussing the particulars, Luke closed the phone and shot a quick glance at Kate who sat with her hands clasped in her lap, eyes glued to the scenery in front of them. "We'll get through this."

She nodded and he couldn't help but remember that drive out of her neighborhood when she was practically comatose with fear.

They'd get through this. They had to.

That night, Luke leaned back in his chair with his feet on the wrought iron railing of the balcony at the hotel and took a sip of Glenlivet. Beside him, Eric smoked a cigar, while Kate slept in the next room. The silence stretched taut between the two men and for the first time in almost twenty years, Luke craved a smoke. He hadn't smoked since the night Dave Jenkins was killed by the four-wheeler.

"So what's the plan?" Eric asked, studying the tip of his

glowing cigar.

"Tomorrow I'll show you the layout of the house. Once you and Kate get into the party—"

"That's not what I meant." Eric looked toward the White House all lit up and the hundreds of headlights cruising down the road below them. "I meant, what's the plan with my sister?"

His voice was smooth as silk but it didn't fool Luke one bit. He'd been expecting this confrontation and dreading it at the same time. The drive up in John's pickup hadn't been an easy one. He'd felt the weight of responsibility crushing him and had automatically withdrawn. He needed the distance to focus. Or so he told himself.

Truth was, he was scared to death. Never before had a mission been so personal. Never before had it involved someone he loved so much.

"I asked you a question, Barone."

Luke wanted to tell Eric to get lost, that what was between he and Kate would stay that way. "I love her."

Eric snorted, the cigar clenched between his teeth. "Like you did the last time?"

Luke winced, even though he deserved the barb. "Kate and I have worked through that."

Eric pulled the cigar from his mouth and tapped it on the railing. Glowing orange ashes floated out of sight, disintegrating on the wind. Several stories below a car alarm shrieked. Eric raised the cigar and tilted his head back, taking another puff.

Luke sipped his scotch. The ice clinking against the side of the crystal glass was the only thing that broke the tense silence.

"You mess with her again and I'll come after you, Barone. I don't care where you hide this time. Got it?"

Luke grabbed hold of his anger before he lost control of it.

He didn't take kindly to threats, but he'd absorb this one for Kate's sake. "Got it."

Eric snuffed out his cigar in the ashtray and rose, stretching his arms above his head. "I'm going to bed." He turned to go, then turned back. "I pulled in a few favors to get the invites to this thing. You owe me big." He walked off, leaving Luke alone with the lingering scent of the cigar and the night noises of a city settling down for the evening.

Except for the lines around his mouth and the grief lodged in his eyes, Kate's brother hadn't changed much. They used to be close, he and Eric, but Luke hadn't expected that closeness to remain and he hadn't been disappointed. He imagined the only thing that had kept Eric from beating on him was Kate's presence and the fact Luke had kept her alive so far. He didn't want to imagine what Eric would do to him if something happened to Kate. He didn't want to imagine what *he* would do.

Something was wrong. He could feel it deep inside, that feeling he never questioned, and had never been wrong. The Carmichaels were in deep with the Saudis, but he wondered if there wasn't more to the story. Kate had questioned Suzanne's motives and Luke discovered that he too found it hard to comprehend Suzanne would kill him for that reason alone. He needed more information and the only place left to get them was inside the Carmichaels' home.

He finished the last of the Glenlivet and rose. He wasn't tired, but he'd go to bed and hold Kate. He took one last glance at the full moon shining down on the most powerful city in the world. The next time the moon shined down on them, they'd both be in the lion's den.

Suzanne slipped into her ice-blue Vera Wang and smoothed the silk over her flat stomach. Thank God she'd never had kids. She hated those pooches of fat moms carried around with their screaming brats. Though there were times she wished she'd had at least one kid. Voters loved politicians with families. She leaned forward and checked her mascara, then pursed her lips and layered on a pale rose lip-gloss. Stepping back, she surveyed the full effect of her ensemble. Perfect. With her hair in an upsweep and the aquamarines around her neck and in her ears, she looked successful but not ostentatious. She patted her hair one last time.

Bradley stood at the makeshift bar on the other side of the room. He'd been sliding downhill ever since Lucas escaped with Katherine McAuley and no amount of sweet talk could bring him out of his funk. He needed to get his act together. Unfortunately, he blamed her for everything, claiming it was because she couldn't find Lucas that he'd started drinking.

Bull. He was weak. And she hated weak people. Especially weak men. And it ticked her off that Bradley was so unappreciative of what she'd done. Because of him, Stuben was dead. Because of him, she'd implemented a nationwide manhunt for Katherine McAuley. Because of him, her best operative was on the run and probably figuring out all her dirty little secrets.

Two bozos in Tennessee suffered fatal injuries because their boat blew up as they stopped to refuel. All because of Bradley who stood at the window and sipped his scotch as if he had not one care in the world. If the voters only knew what she'd done to get him where he was today. Hell, they should elect *her* president.

The door to their suite opened and Suzanne's assistant poked her head in. Her gaze darted to Bradley, then back to Suzanne.

"A minute, Mrs. Carmichael?"

"If it's about the caterer, you take care of it."

Jessica shook her head. "No." Her gaze flicked to Bradley again. "It's about the information you requested."

Suzanne glanced at Bradley, who stared blankly out the window, a crystal glass clenched in his hand. He'd be okay for the moment, but soon she'd have to take the alcohol away from him. Still fuming, she walked out of the room, closing the door behind her as Jessica handed her a piece of paper.

"A call came in to the Cincinnati police department about an abandoned car a few blocks from McAuley's home."

Suzanne took the piece of paper. It contained the description and license plate number of a dark blue Ford Explorer.

"A man by the name of Jay Lang rented it."

Suzanne searched her mind for the name Jay Lang and came up with nothing. "A Jay Lang rented that same Explorer at Ronald Reagan Airport a few days before," Jessica continued.

Her heart began to accelerate. She crumpled the paper, then patted her hair with a shaking hand. A smile broke across her face. She had a name. Jay Lang.

"Find out if this Jay Lang has credit cards and if he's used them recently. If you discover *anything*, notify me."

Luke drew back the slide on his Glock, checked the round, then holstered it at his back. Due to tight security, Eric wouldn't carry his weapon so Luke would be the only one with firepower. He didn't like it but he would play by the rules. For now.

Eric stood in front of the mirror adjusting the bow tie on his tux while Kate stood at the door.

He'd been right. Dressed to the nines, no one would recognize her as the same bohemian in the pictures the news media was flashing all over the place. Tonight she was classic elegance. Suave sophistication with hair piled on top of her head, lips painted a berry red, eyes smoky and sexy. He should have bought her a less seductive dress, but when he'd seen it at the store, he knew she would look fabulous in it. Black silk clung to slim her hips and dipped between rounded breasts.

"Ready?" he asked, turning to Eric instead of Kate, wanting so badly to take her in his arms, to run away forever. Except they'd tried that and it hadn't worked.

Eric stepped away from the mirror, looked his sister up and down, then frowned. He still hated this idea, Luke knew. But Eric also understood the reasoning. Would have agreed with it too if it hadn't been his sister walking into the viper pit with him. "Ready," he said.

With a nod, Luke left the room first, unable to help himself when he trailed a finger down Kate's bare arm. He didn't look at her as he walked away. It would devastate his already-crumbling defenses and he needed all the strength he could muster for what lay ahead.

Eric and Kate would wait fifteen minutes then follow him out. They wouldn't see each other again until Eric opened the window to the Carmichaels' study.

Every window was lit, soft music drifted from the open front door while laughter and the clink of silverware and crystal mingled with the scent of roses. Eric and Kate walked up the stone walkway, Eric's hand at her elbow. Her heels clicked a light staccato that sounded suspiciously like a death knell. They hadn't spoken more than two words since leaving the hotel. Kate couldn't manage to get anything past the terror strangling her.

At the door, Eric presented their invitations. The hulk of a security man, with an earpiece and a suit that barely stretched across linebacker shoulders, studied the cream vellum for a long time. So long Kate got dizzy from holding her breath. A squeeze of her elbow from Eric reminded her to gulp in a lungful of air.

The guard squinted up at Eric and barely gave Kate a passing glance before waving them through. She would have breathed a sigh of relief. If she'd been relieved.

Eric glanced at his watch as they descended into the horde.

Luke had told her what to expect but it didn't come close to the reality. She felt like an extra on the set of *Dallas* or *Dynasty*. The crystal chandeliers competed with the glitter of the jewelry around women's necks, wrists and on their ears. But unlike a television set, Kate doubted these jewels were fake. Groups mingled, broke up and came together again. Men in black tuxedos bent their heads toward each other as if discussing major world policy. Which they probably were.

"Act like you've been there and done that," Eric said out the side of his mouth.

"I don't think that's possible considering I've never been here or done anything like this."

He smiled and it eased her apprehension somewhat. All they had to do was act as if they belonged for the next twenty minutes, then find their way to the study, let Luke in and he'd do his thing.

Piece of cake. Not.

However, before she knew it, Eric was tugging on her hand. "Time to go," he said. They wove through the crowd, Kate's hand held tightly in her brother's, until they came to a closed door that, when Eric opened it, dumped them into a hushed hallway. A waiter rushed by balancing a tray loaded with crystal flutes of champagne. Another hustled by with an empty tray and a harried look. Neither paid them any mind.

For the first time since entering the plush Carmichael home, Kate breathed easy.

A flutter of movement out of the corner of her eye caught Suzanne's attention. Her assistant stood in a side door, motioning to her.

Suzanne touched the arm of the woman she'd been talking to. For the life of her, she couldn't remember the other lady's name. "If you would excuse me a moment, I think there's a crisis in the kitchen."

The woman laughed and waved a hand in the air. "Oh, the duties of a hostess. When you become first lady, you won't have those worries."

Suzanne smiled wider. "One can only hope and pray—" The woman's name came to her in a flash. "—Mrs. Foster." Suzanne stepped away and wove through the crowd. When she reached the door, she took one last look around and slid out of the room. She held up her hand to silence Jessica as she caught sight of a couple walking down the hall toward them.

The man was exceptionally tall with broad shoulders, a tapering waist and slim hips. His tux fit as if custom-tailored. That wasn't uncommon in this crowd, but the way he filled it out was. His wheat blond hair was trimmed short and piercing blue eyes met hers. He nodded as he approached, heading toward the kitchen.

But those penetrating eyes of his pierced her with their intensity. Something flickered in them. Hate? Impossible. She didn't even know this man, but her hands started to sweat anyway.

"I seem to have lost my way," he said in a deep baritone that matched his impressive physique. Suzanne eyed the stranger and pointed to the door leading to the heart of the party. "That way, Mr..." She let her voice trail off into a question.

The woman stood silently beside him, her gaze sweeping over Suzanne, but Suzanne ignored her.

Amusement lightened eyes that crinkled at the corners. He held out his hand. "Just call me Mac. Sorry for the intrusion."

"Not a problem...Mac." She shook the warm, calloused hand. "I'm Suzanne Carmichael."

"Oh, I know who you are, Ms. Carmichael."

She shivered at the innocent words that for some reason seemed menacing. Mac and the woman slipped through the door.

"Did you learn anything else?" Suzanne asked Jessica, reluctantly tearing her gaze from the door.

"Jay Lang rented two rooms at the Wyndham."

Suzanne darted a look at the door the blond couple just walked through. The Wyndham was a mere mile or so away.

Lucas was in town. And so, apparently, was Kate.

Chapter Fourteen

"Oh my God. Oh my God." Kate's stomach turned flips as Eric hustled her through the crowd before finding a place behind a group of boisterous partygoers. She slumped against the wall, pressing her sweaty palms against the cool wallpaper.

"Stand up straight," Eric said, his gaze bouncing around the room.

She straightened and tried to slow the erratic beat of her heart. "That was close."

"Too close. But damn if Barone wasn't right. Hiding you right under Suzanne's nose was brilliant."

Kate glanced around at the people closest to them. Tonight was meant for hobnobbing, glad-handing and brown-nosing. No one expected a fugitive to be in their midst. Yeah, pretty brilliant on Luke's part. Slowly her heart slowed, the light that had dimmed in her panic brightened and her tunnel vision cleared. She never wanted to be that scared again.

"There she is," Eric said, turning so he faced her, his body blocking any view Suzanne would have of her. When Suzanne stepped into the crowd, he grabbed Kate's hand. "Come on."

Once again they made their way to the side door and slipped through. This time no one stopped them as they hustled toward the study.

✧

The window to the study slid open. Luke glanced around the dark, side yard before throwing one leg over the sill, then the other.

"Took you long enough," he said as he plopped down on the other side and Eric lowered the window. He scanned the room before his gaze landed on Kate's frightened face.

"Ran into a small SNAFU," Eric said, following him to the computer.

With the tap of a button, the computer whirred to life. "Oh?" He glanced up at Kate again and frowned. She was entirely too pale and her body trembled. But like a good little soldier, she was holding up. "What happened?"

"The Carmichael woman was in the hall. She's a piece of work."

Luke grunted as the screen flashed. He had to force his gaze back to the computer.

"I felt like a mouse in the jaws of a cat," Eric was saying.

"Did she get a look at Kate?" Again his gaze went to her. Large, dark eyes stared back.

"Not really," she said, and he was glad to hear her voice was strong. "She only noticed Eric."

He searched her face. "You okay?"

She flashed him a bright smile that didn't fool him. "Peachy."

The computer beeped, then asked for a password. "Get her back to the hotel," he said to Eric, then to Kate he softened his voice. "I'll see you there."

She sent him a crooked smile before they slid out the door

and he set to work.

Kate understood Luke was under enormous pressure. That he was doing this for them. So they could lead a normal life when all this was over. Still, she'd wanted so badly to lay her head against his chest, to hear his heart beat beneath her ear and close her eyes for just a second.

Instead she was walking back into the lion's den and hopefully out the door.

"Ready?" Eric studied her, hand on the knob before he led them back into the party.

She squared her shoulders, adjusted her gown then nodded. "Ready."

"This time it's easy as pie. Just walk out the door."

Right. Walk out the door. She could do that.

Eric opened the door and she stepped through, no longer in awe of the flash of wealth, but rather disgusted with it and the insincerity of the people present.

Eric placed a hand at her back as they headed for the door. She kept her eye on the bouncer who surveyed the crowd with a jaundiced eye, hands clasped behind his back. Her gaze wandered farther, to the opened door and the trees she could barely glimpse just beyond.

"Eric McAuley?"

Eric gripped her hip and she stopped, afraid to turn around, afraid to see who had recognized her brother. Afraid whoever it was would recognize her.

Slowly she turned and let out a relieved breath. Eric shook hands with the man she didn't recognize, taking his other hand off her for a moment. A couple pushed between them. A group walked by and before Kate knew it, she couldn't see her brother. She panicked, her heart racing as she glanced around the room. The door. She had to make it to the door. If she could leave, she'd be okay. She'd meet up with Eric at the car.

She turned, but rough hands grabbed her upper arms. "Please, Ms. McAuley, if you would come with us." It wasn't a request, neither a demand. It just was. And there was no arguing.

She opened her mouth to scream, determined she wasn't going anywhere without making some sort of scene, but fingers dug into her arm and her scream turned into a whimper of pain. She struggled, trying to pull her arm free and drove the stiletto of one shoe into the toe of a polished loafer. The man easily sidestepped as another crowded close. Something hard pressed against her side and she went still, her blood turning to ice. She'd never had a gun shoved into her before but it was a feeling she instinctively recognized.

She weighed the prospect of continuing her struggle. Would they shoot her in this crowd? Probably, if they could explain it away by identifying her as the armed and dangerous criminal the entire nation was searching for. And she couldn't let that happen with Luke in the house.

The fight draining out of her, she let them lead her back to the hallway where she stumbled through the door and looked up into the face of Suzanne Carmichael.

"Katherine McAuley. How very smart of you to hide in my home. Among my guests." Suzanne's sneer told Kate that while the woman might be impressed, she wasn't pleased. "I must say, I didn't recognize you at first. Where is your lovely escort?"

Kate pursed her lips together. No way would she give up Eric to this woman.

Suzanne's eyes narrowed to deadly slits. "Come with me." She pivoted and walked away. Kate's knees threatened to give out and she cast a glance in either direction, ready to run. Two doors down, Luke worked on the computer, but she couldn't alert Suzanne to his presence.

The guards grabbed her arms and dragged her forward. Kate's gaze swept the hallway looking for an escape route, a fire alarm to pull, anything to warn Luke and Eric. As they rounded a corner and headed up a set of steps, Kate glanced behind her and locked gazes with a pair of angry blue eyes.

If looks could kill, the one Eric shot her would have done the job nicely.

Luke sat back as the computer copied the files onto the memory stick he'd brought. He tried to wrap his mind around all he'd just discovered, but his stunned brain couldn't grasp the far-reaching consequences of the Carmichaels' actions. Rage tore through him, making him want to throw back his head and howl. With the rage came pain and a sense of denial. But, no, he couldn't deny what he'd just seen. It was all there, in black and white, the implications horrendous.

Shaking with his fury, barely able to see straight, he stood and paced as the computer whirred behind him and the muffled laughter of hundreds of people two rooms over drifted to him. He could barely breathe, but it wasn't the lack of air choking him. It was the deception.

He closed his eyes against the pain and the incredible sense of betrayal. The computer beeped, signaling it had finished saving, but he didn't move. Couldn't move.

Betrayed. He'd been betrayed.

He strode toward the desk and the computer, but before he could reach it, the door burst open and Luke froze in the shadows. Eric stomped in and flipped on the lights, illuminating the room and temporarily blinding Luke. He raised his arm as if to ward off the light. "What the—"

"They have Kate," Eric said, his face a mask of fury.

"What?"

Eric turned steely blue eyes to Luke. "When this is over, I'm gonna kill her."

"Kill who?" He couldn't move, his feet glued to the floor and his mind uncharacteristically sluggish. He hadn't thought he could be any more surprised tonight. Not after what he'd just learned. Who had Kate? His stomach lurched as foreboding twisted through him. "Damn it, McAuley, what the hell's going on?"

Pain seeped through the anger on Eric's face. "Suzanne Carmichael has Kate. I couldn't follow without them noticing me."

Kate swallowed as the dismissed security guards left with orders to locate her brother. She tried to hide her panic, finding she was more afraid for Luke and Eric than herself.

She'd been taken into what looked like the Carmichaels' bedroom suite. A tall, four-poster bed took up one wall, windows another and doors led off the third wall. Kate eyed them with escape not far from her thoughts.

"Where's Lucas?"

Kate's gaze swung back to Suzanne. "I don't know."

Suzanne strode forward, and without warning, backhanded Kate across the cheek. Her head snapped back, tears stung her eyes and stars danced across her vision. She bit her tongue and the coppery taste of blood seeped into her mouth. She blinked away the tears of pain.

"Liar." Suzanne turned and sauntered away.

Terrified, a cold fist closed over Kate's heart, squeezing. Squeezing. She edged toward the door.

"Don't even think about running," Suzanne said, her back still to Kate. "My men are just outside and have orders to shoot." She turned and pinned Kate with a cool look. "I know all about you," she went on. "I know Lucas is traveling under the name Jay Lang. If you don't tell me where he is, I'll find him anyway." She advanced, a sneer twisting her rose-tinted lips. "But at what cost to you, Katherine?"

Kate's cheek burned, her knees felt like rubber and she was terrified she'd collapse. But she refused to back down.

Suzanne grabbed Kate's hand in a gentle gesture, lifting it and examining her short, unpainted nails. She tried to tug her hand loose, but Suzanne was stronger. She tightened her hold and stroked the top of Kate's hand. Unable to hold her fear in, Kate shivered. Suzanne's smile would have frozen the boiling pits of hell and Kate began to shake all over. That fist around her heart increased its pressure until she could feel each unsteady beat through her rib cage.

"Such pretty hands. I've seen the art these hands create. Such a pity if I had to ruin them."

Oh, God, no! Not her hands. Suzanne squeezed until Kate's fingers turned white. Her knuckles ground into one another. She bit back a whimper, refusing to lend voice to her very real fear. Clutching her bottom lip between her teeth, the waves of pain rolled over her, traveling up her arm.

"Tell me where he is, Katherine." Suzanne's soft, menacing voice drifted around Kate, stealing into her brain. Her fingers went numb while her hand screamed in pain. She blinked tears away. Suzanne Carmichael could smash every one of her fingers, could crush the bones in her hand, make it impossible for her to paint, but Kate would never admit Luke was in this house. A wave of nausea washed through her and she closed her eyes, then snapped them open, too afraid to let the woman out of her sight.

Pulling on a reserve of courage she didn't know she possessed, Kate pulled her free arm back and let it fly. Quick as lightening, Suzanne twisted, bringing Kate's arm behind her back and yanking up. Kate gasped, the pain robbing her of speech and breath. She bent forward to ease the pain but Suzanne followed the movement, increasing her pressure until Kate thought for sure her arm would snap.

"Where is he?" Suzanne's breath whispered across her neck, sending gooseflesh tingling down her spine.

Kate's breaths came shallow and short.

"Answer me, Katherine."

The words were soft, the tone hard, and Kate's fear rose to a new level. She couldn't pull in enough air to satisfy her brain's need for oxygen. Afraid she'd pass out, she took to gulping, but that didn't help. Black dots danced before her eyes. She needed to get a grip. She needed to calm down. To focus through the pain.

Miraculously, Suzanne let go, pushing Kate forward as she did. Kate cried out and stumbled but caught herself from falling. Suzanne suddenly stood before her, a sneer marring the perfection of her face. She slapped Kate, the back of her wedding band cutting into Kate's cheek. Kate raised her good hand to touch the spot, stared at the bright red blood on her fingers as her arm throbbed and her other hand began to swell. She hurt all over and knew this wasn't the end. Suzanne was toying with her, terrorizing her until she decided Kate's life wasn't worth the thrill anymore.

She straightened and tensed, refusing to give in. Suzanne sauntered over to a small dressing table, opened the drawer and pulled out a gun. Kate's gaze riveted to the weapon, the same type Luke carried. Her mouth went dry. The black silk of her dress clung to her through the sweat coating her back.

Suzanne screwed on a longer metal piece, then pulled the slide back. The metallic click reverberated through the quiet room. Kate's heart beat hard, Her breath came in small gasps. Blood pounded in her ears. Suzanne raised the gun and Kate stared down the barrel.

Her life didn't flash before her like in all the books. In fact, she couldn't pull up one clear memory of anything. The world slowed to a crawl. Somewhere a clock ticked the seconds by as the soft music of a harp drifted from the lower level. People's voices floated to her. A car honked a few streets over. Some bizarre part of her mind registered that outside, people's lives went on as normal. As if hers weren't about to end.

"What do you know about me?" Suzanne asked.

Kate stared at the woman, her mind a complete blank.

Suzanne waved the gun from side to side. "What has Lucas told you about me?"

Kate couldn't remember. The entire reason they were here eluded her! Her mouth went dry and she hadn't thought it possible to fear more. But she did. Her hand throbbed and she had to tense her muscles to remain upright.

"Come now, Ms. McAuley, he had to have told you something."

"Oil." It was the only word she could force from her tight throat.

Suzanne raised a perfectly waxed blonde eyebrow. "So he

figured that out, did he? I told Bradley making that deal with Zamal was a mistake. What else did he tell you?"

Kate's mind buzzed and she resisted the urge to rub her temples. What else? What else? There wasn't anything else, yet Suzanne looked at her, expecting more. Was there more? Was there something she and Luke missed? Her gaze strayed to the gun. Such a small thing and it could end her life. Never to see Luke again, never to hold him, to tell him she loved him. She swayed. The gun wavered. Blood dripped onto her dress from the cut on her cheek. Her hand throbbed with the beat of her heart. This was it. The end. *I love you, Luke.*

But something deep inside, some inner fortitude she hadn't counted on, reared up and took hold. She would *not* die like this, not like a scared rabbit, afraid to move. *Run!* Her legs gained strength and she lunged for the door just as it flew open. Luke stood in the opening, his gun sweeping the room, stopping on Suzanne. His shoulders filled the doorway and Kate sobbed with relief as she stumbled to a halt.

Suzanne pointed the gun toward Luke.

The blank screen of Kate's mind suddenly filled with images, dozens of them. Luke falling through her open door, bloody and beaten. Luke holding her as she cried in his arms. Luke caring for her in the hotel room. Luke rising above her as he plunged inside her. Where once there had been no memories, there were now too many.

And Kate refused to relinquish them to Suzanne Carmichael, refused to live her life with mere memories of a slice of time carved out of this bizarre scenario.

"It's too late, Suzanne," Luke said.

"I don't think so, Barone."

"I know everything." He emphasized the word everything and Suzanne flinched. Luke took a small step forward, head tilted, arms locked, gun pointed at Suzanne. Eric stood completely still in the doorway. "Everything," Luke repeated, softly this time, his gaze never leaving Suzanne's.

"I doubt that," she said, but her voice didn't sound so sure.

Kate's gaze swung wildly from Suzanne to Luke. It was almost as if they had forgotten all about her, that some silent, hidden conversation was taking place.

"I know about Peru." Luke's voice was strained. The muscles in his jaw twitched.

Suzanne shook her head, but the fanatic light in her eyes went out. "No, you don't."

"The information's already on its way to the White House."

With a cry of rage, Suzanne locked her elbows.

"No!" Kate lurched for Luke, stumbled on the hem of her gown and fell forward.

The gun went off with a soft *pffft*, quickly followed by a loud bang. A force hit her in the side, throwing her off balance. She stumbled again, her knees collapsing under her. Luke's mouth opened in a cry, his face draining of color. He grabbed for her, their fingers sliding against each other, then apart.

Eric burst forward, grabbing Suzanne as she slithered to the floor, blood splattered across her gown and face.

Kate fell to the soft carpet. Pain speared through her, beginning and ending nowhere, yet everywhere. Her head pounded; her legs lost all feeling. A numbness seeped through her, stealing her breath. Luke knelt beside her. His lips moved, but she couldn't hear anything. Blackness surrounded her, weighed her down, pulled her in. She closed her eyes and pictured the houseboat and a perfect summer day with cicadas buzzing and birds chirping. She sat on the dive deck, the water gently lapping at her feet, Rembrandt curled on her lap, Luke swimming lazy circles in front of her.

"I love you, Katie. Don't go," he said, his expression sad.

She frowned. "Go where?"

Tears spilled from his eyes, dripped down his cheeks and became one with the lake. "Don't leave me."

She opened her mouth to say "never", but she'd lost the use of her voice. Then she couldn't hear the birds or the cicadas. The lake disappeared and Luke was gone too. Nothing remained but the all-consuming pain.

And the grief.

Chapter Fifteen

Luke dropped to his knees and slid a hand under Kate's head, gently lifting it. A large stain spread across her torso, soaking into the cream-colored carpet beneath her. "Kate?" His voice came out in a hoarse whisper. He pressed a hand to her side to stem the flow of blood. Instantly his fingers were covered in blood. Her blood. Kate's blood. A numbing pain stole through him and spread from his feet to his head. No. He wouldn't lose her. Not now. Not after finding her again. He wouldn't allow it.

People crowded the room, but Luke blocked them from his mind. She still breathed. Her chest rose and fell, but not like it should. Too slow. He grabbed her hand and squeezed her fingers. Cold. She was so cold. Tears blurred his vision. He shouldn't move her. Didn't know what damage had been done. But he wanted to hold her next to him. Because she was cold. And she needed warmth. If she was warm she'd wake up.

Eric knelt beside him and took Kate's other hand. He pressed his fingers to the pulse in her wrist. His worried gaze met Luke's, but Luke looked away. "She'll be fine," he said. "She'll be fine."

Eric patted him on the shoulder and said something, but Luke didn't listen. He squeezed her fingers again, silently willing her to squeeze back. Nothing. No response. Hands tugged at his shoulders, but he shrugged them away. Voices spoke from a distance, but he ignored them. People walked around, but he wouldn't lift his head to see who.

"Luke. The paramedics are here." Eric pulled on his shoulders again and pried his fingers from Kate's. Her hand dropped to the floor, lifeless. Luke rose but his legs couldn't support his weight; he sagged and Eric held him up. The paramedics stepped in, obstructing his view of her.

No! His mind screamed in pain, but he wouldn't give voice to the shout of horror. She'd survive. She had to.

As they placed her on a stretcher, a lock of hair fell over her eyes and Luke wanted to brush it away, but they wouldn't let him get close enough. They began to wheel her away. When Luke tried to follow, Eric held him back.

"You need to stay here." He tilted his head toward the police officers looking on with sympathy. The director of the CIA stood next to Suzanne. Luke's gaze touched on everyone. He knew his duty. He needed to pass on the information he'd learned before more lives were taken, more operatives were betrayed like he and John had been.

"I'll go with Kate," Eric said. "I'll call you as soon as I know something." He paused, then squeezed Luke's arm looking concerned. "Will you be okay?"

Luke nodded, then shook off the numbness threatening to pull him under. Kate's shooting wouldn't be for nothing. They'd come to discover the truth and he'd found so much more. His superiors needed to know what had happened.

Eric shot him another concerned look, then headed out the door, following the stretcher. Luke turned to Howard Rafferty, the director of the CIA, a man known for his fairness and his ruthlessness. Luke was counting on the ruthlessness.

"I'll tell you everything I know. In the car on the way to the hospital."

The man nodded. "We can ride in my limo."

Luke ran a weary, shaking hand down his face. He'd been inside the limo, answering the director's questions, for over an hour. His thoughts were beginning to fragment. His sentences became disjointed.

The limo driver had been calling the hospital every fifteen minutes for updates. Kate had been rushed into surgery twenty minutes ago. There was nothing he could do but wait. And worry. And pray. But he couldn't pray with the director shooting questions at him like bullets from a sub-machine gun.

"So let me get this straight," Rafferty said. "Just one more time, then you can go," he added after Luke's sigh of exasperation.

Luke looked out the tinted window at the hospital all lit up in the night sky. Somewhere in one of those rooms lay Kate, a bullet in her side, fighting for her life.

"You were at the Carmichaels' for a small dinner party and overheard Bradley talking with Hazim Zamal—"

"I didn't overhear anything. I walked outside to get some fresh air, saw them talking and left. I was never close enough to hear anything. My thought is that Bradley assumed I heard something and in a panic ran to Suzanne."

Rafferty made some notes on his pad of paper. "So you left the Carmichaels' and went to a bar, correct?"

Luke nodded, still staring out the window. Suzanne was also in that hospital, but the reports they'd received said her injury was minor and she would be released the next day. Where was the fairness in that? How could God let Kate suffer, possibly die, while Suzanne lived? Guilt didn't even come close to the emotion he felt right now. Despair, desolation, anguish, those came a little closer, but not much. He should have been the one lying on that table, not Kate. If he'd done his job right, if he hadn't knocked on her front door and pulled her into this web of conspiracy, she would be alive and well and whole.

The director tapped him on the shoulder and Luke turned.

"She's in surgery, Barone, she won't even know you're not there." Rafferty's tone was sympathetic and apologetic but also conveyed that Luke wasn't getting out of the limo anytime soon. His wife had died two years ago and since then he'd devoted his life to his career. Luke didn't want to be like that. He wanted more than work. He wanted Kate. "You went to a bar and what?"

Luke forced his mind back to that night. Rafferty was right. Kate was in surgery and there was nothing he could do but wait. Might as well get this over with so when she did wake up he could be there for her.

"I went to the bar for a few drinks, then walked home. I noticed my security system had been turned off but by then it was too late. I was grabbed, dragged inside and beaten. I think it was supposed to appear as if I'd walked in on a burglary, fought the intruders and died in the process."

Rafferty nodded, looking thoughtful. "That would be my guess too. Stopping at the bar gave Suzanne time to get her men in place."

Luke nodded absently and told the rest of the story, how he'd run to Kate, shot Stuben and gone on the run. How by chance he discovered Bradley's connection to Zamal while he and Kate hid out on the houseboat. "I wasn't positive that's what was going on," he said. "But it seemed likely that Bradley and Zamal were in deep with price fixing. That's what I wanted to prove." Yet he'd found so much more.

"I'm sorry," Rafferty said. "I'm sure this is quite a blow to you."

If only he knew.

Rafferty cleared his throat. "My guess is Suzanne was afraid you would leak the information about Zamal, then an investigation would reveal her sale of weapons to the People of Light. These days the American people don't take treason lightly, especially when it involves terrorists. And they sure as heck wouldn't vote the Carmichaels into office."

Funny how Luke had never even suspected that Suzanne was the one who had sent he and John into the Peruvian jungle as a decoy. He pinched the bridge of his nose and closed his eyes. "What I can't figure out is why. Why, when she has the world in her hands, would Suzanne sell weapons to known terrorists? Why would Bradley, on the brink of becoming president of the United States, make such an underhanded deal?"

Rafferty shrugged. "Power. Money. It's a potent combination that steals people's common sense. We may never know why. She's going down, Barone. You did good."

"Yeah." But he didn't feel like it, not while Kate was fighting for her life.

Rafferty clapped him on the shoulder. "Go to your woman. You've got until tomorrow morning, then I need you back. I'd give you more time if I could..."

Luke nodded. "I understand." And he did. The department needed him. Needed his knowledge to wade through the vast amount of information he'd gleaned from the Carmichaels' computer. But that didn't mean he liked it.

The car door opened and Luke climbed out, his legs shaking from exhaustion and fear, and reached back in to shake his boss's hand. "I'll be here in the morning. Pick me up at nine."

The director nodded. Luke stepped away and turned toward

the hospital doors.

When he entered the waiting room, Eric stood, his expression solemn. Luke's heart skipped a beat, an unspoken question hovering on his lips, refusing to lend voice to his fear.

"Her colon was nicked," Eric said. "They're patching it up now. They say the threat of infection is what we have to worry about."

If she survived the surgery, he'd worry about the rest later. *Please, God, let her survive.* He'd bargain anything, everything, to keep her alive, but all he had was Kate. "H-How long will the surgery take?"

"A few hours. I need to call my parents, Luke. Can I leave you alone?"

Luke raised his head. "Yeah. I need to call John, anyway." He had to tell John all he knew. The man deserved that.

Other than telling Kate about Peru, it was the hardest conversation he'd ever had. He started off by telling John about Kate, barely able to force the words past his throat. But John and Luke had worked together for a long time and John finally told Luke to spill the rest of the story.

"Suzanne Carmichael was selling American weapons to the People of Light." There was a long silence and Luke forged on. "She sent you into the jungles of Peru, then informed the leaders of your whereabouts. Her superiors were on her back to shut down the terrorist organization, yet she had a huge deal coming up she couldn't postpone. So she played both sides. I'm sorry, man." Luke's heart went out to his best friend. He'd been sacrificed by a rogue agent, suffered months and months of torture because one woman turned her back on her country for financial gain.

Luke's own betrayal was no better. With Rafferty on

Suzanne's case to get Callahan out, she'd called Luke. The arms trading had been finished by then and she'd been ready to step in and play the hero, extracting her agent from her supposed enemy. She hadn't counted on Luke offering himself up as a replacement. And she hadn't counted on the terrorist leaders to hold him for so long. She'd assured Luke he'd be out in twenty-four hours. But the terrorists had turned greedy, wanting more weapons for less money, threatening to expose her to her government. Luke ran a hand down his face and sighed. So much deception. So many lies. So many lives hurt because of Suzanne Carmichael's greed.

"Just so you know," he said, "she's been arrested. After she's released from the hospital she'll be taken to jail."

"Thanks for telling me," John said. Luke tried to determine his state of mind through his words, but like Luke, John was an old hand at deception and Luke couldn't discern a thing, other than the gut feeling that his friend had to be reeling from the betrayal. Just like he was. "I won't say anything. What about the Senator and his dealings with the Saudis?" John asked.

"Got all that information too."

"I'm sure his party's in an uproar now that they don't have a candidate."

Luke agreed, but none of that concerned him. What concerned him was Kate, and how she was faring, and if she survived, and if she would hate him for putting her life on the line.

At the same time Rafferty's limo pulled up to the front doors of the hospital at nine in the morning, Kate was wheeled out of surgery. According to her doctor, she'd done well. Her vitals were strong and now they just had to wait to see if infection would set in. They were transporting her to recovery when Luke climbed back into Rafferty's limo, weary but relieved and angry he couldn't be at her side.

He spent the day with Rafferty and his staff, going over the evidence he'd found in the Carmichaels' home. The news hit hard that America's golden couple were traitors to their own country. Kate's hospital was surrounded by print and television media from all over the world. Rafferty sent men to guard Kate, but Luke wouldn't rest easy until he was by her side. He received updates every half hour. Kate still had not awoken from the surgery and her temperature was rising. The doctors were keeping watch on her, pumping antibiotics into her.

Twelve hours later, Rafferty finally released Luke with a warning to stay close in case they needed him again. The last Kate update had been five minutes before. She drifted in and out of consciousness, but had yet to speak. Luke raced to the hospital. It'd been over twenty-four hours since he'd showered. He'd been in the same clothes for the same amount of time, but he couldn't waste precious minutes showering and changing.

The throng of media was incredible. Police had roped off the front of the building, keeping the hounds at bay, but it was still a circus and impossible to get the taxi through. Luke hopped out, threw the driver some bills and sprinted for the entrance. Cameras whirred and clicked. Reporters called out his name, shouting questions about his relationship with Kate and the Carmichaels. He ignored them as he slid under the police tape.

When he reached the door to Kate's room, he discovered the media was nothing compared to three very angry McAuley men. Kate's father and her two brothers, Riley and Paul, stood in front of her door, arms crossed over their chests. They were big, intimidating blond men with quick tempers and a strong bond with Kate.

Luke mimicked their poses, crossing his arms over his own chest. "I need to see Kate."

"Like hell," her father said. Riley and Paul nodded.

"Don't make me force my way in. Kate wouldn't like that."

"Get out, Barone. You're not needed here. She has her family with her now."

Luke tamped down on his anger and reminded himself they were only trying to protect Kate. "Look, I know you have some animosity toward me for what happened—" All three men snorted. "—but Kate and I've worked through that. She's forgiven me and we've moved on."

They didn't look convinced. In fact, they looked like they wanted to beat him to a pulp. Luke sighed and ran a hand down his face. He didn't want to do this now. Not without showering and shaving and looking halfway presentable, but he didn't have much choice.

"I wanted to wait before I asked this, but apparently you aren't letting me in there." He tipped his head to the door that led to Kate. His whole body yearned to be with her. He'd swallow any amount of pride to do that, including getting on his knees and begging. "I want to marry Kate, if she'll have me."

Riley's hands fell to his sides as his eyes widened in shock. Paul snorted again and shook his head. Mr. McAuley's face got a pinched, thunderous look. "You've *got* to be kidding me," he sputtered.

Luke flinched. "I deserve that, I know. But Kate understands that what happened eighteen months ago wasn't my fault." Damn Suzanne Carmichael. The woman had ruined his life.

"Oh, please." Paul rolled his eyes. "Get out, Barone. You're not wanted here."

The voices came and went. Her mother's, Paul's, Riley's, her father. Eric. But not the voice she wanted. Not the voice she needed. Every time someone entered her room she'd pull herself up from the black hole that threatened to suck her under forever. She'd fight her way to consciousness, listening for him. But he never came.

And each time, she'd sink back down into the darkness. Each time she'd float farther from the light. Her body burned and sometimes she wondered if she were in hell. Maybe she didn't deserve heaven—after all she was no saint—but she didn't think she deserved hell either.

Surely that's where she was. Hot. Everything was hot. And with the heat came pain. Piercing pain in her side, as if she'd been split in half and not put together right. In the darkness there was no pain. The voices of the people she knew and loved called to her, begged her to return to them. But the one voice remained silent.

Absent.

"I'm asking for your permission to marry your daughter."

"Denied." Mr. McAuley's angry gaze burned through Luke. He wasn't surprised at the answer, but it still hurt. He'd simply keep trying. He'd prove to the McAuley men he was worthy of their sister and daughter. And he would marry her. If she'd have him. But to do that, he needed to get through that door.

Salvation arrived in the form of Kate's oldest brother and mother. Eric approached from the left while Kate's mother stepped out of Kate's room. Luke craned his neck to get a glimpse of Kate but all he saw was the foot of the hospital bed before Riley stepped into his line of sight.

Mrs. McAuley appeared tired and worn out, her usually bright blue eyes dulled with worry and grief. She glimpsed Luke and a small smile tugged at the corners of her mouth. Eric stepped up beside Luke and for once Luke appreciated the support. Over the last twenty-four hours, the oldest McAuley brother and Luke had formed a special bond.

"Hello, Luke."

Luke tipped his head to Kate's mother. "Mrs. McAuley."

The woman eyed all four of her men, taking in the threatening, obstinate poses of the three blocking the door. "What's going on here?" she asked.

Mr. McAuley tipped his head to Luke. "He wants in."

"So let him in."

"Hell no!" Her husband looked at her in shock.

She smacked him on the arm, then proceeded down the line, smacking her two sons. "Let him in. Kate hasn't responded to any of us. Maybe she'll respond to him."

Hadn't responded? He barely controlled the urge to push through the obstinate family.

Eric stepped forward. "Let him in. Luke and I have an understanding. If he hurts Kate again, he's mine."

Not the most ringing endorsement, but it would have to do. The three men moved, grudgingly, shooting him murderous looks. Luke pushed the door open and stepped into Kate's room.

The door closed with a quiet click. He stayed where he was, unable to venture in. She lay so still under the covers, her arms at her sides, the machines beeping around her. A nasty cut ran down one cheek. Her skin was pale as milk, her blonde hair fanned out over the pillow. Her chest rose and fell in a steady rhythm that reassured him. He stepped up and touched her hand. The fingers were swollen, bloated. What had Suzanne done to her? That familiar rage that had been building ever since he read with horror the atrocities and double-dealings Suzanne Carmichael was involved in, threatened to escape. He stomped it back down. Not here. Not now.

He rounded the bed and took her other hand in his. An IV ran from the top of her hand to a bag hanging by her head. Tears formed in his eyes, blurring his vision. This time he let them fall. They dribbled down his cheek, dropped from his chin and landed on the blanket covering her. "Katie?"

Chapter Sixteen

"Katie?"

Something inside her responded, telling her to wake up, to open her eyes. No, not inside her. Outside her. The voice. The voice prodded her slumbering conscious.

"Open your eyes, Kate. Look at me."

She turned away, afraid of the pain.

"Come back to me, Kate."

The voice. The one she'd been searching for. The one that'd been absent. She reached down deep, found a hidden strength and began to swim toward the voice.

"I love you, Kate."

The pain came in dull throbs, not as sharp or as intense as before. Her eyelids fluttered open, then closed. Light. The light hurt. "Luke?"

"Right here, angel."

His fingers squeezed hers and she tried to smile but didn't know if she'd succeeded. She opened her eyes again and caught a glimpse of him before they shut on their own. "You...look like...hell."

His laughter was soft and it made her heart flutter.

"I'm hot."

"It's the fever. The doctor's are working to bring it down."

"Milkshake." Man, a milkshake sounded wonderful. Cold, wet. "Vanilla."

He laughed again. She loved that sound.

"No." She tried to shake her head but pain stabbed her. "Peanut butter."

"You want a peanut butter milkshake?"

Her tongue darted out to lick dry, cracked lips. "Mmmm."

"Okay, angel. One peanut butter milkshake coming up."

The blackness came fast this time. She didn't want to succumb to it, but had expended all her energy and couldn't fight it anymore. "Love you."

"Love you too, Katie. When you get out of this hospital bed, we're getting married. Okay?"

She nodded and this time she felt the smile spread across her face. "Okay."

"I want to go home."

Kate leaned her head against the chair and sucked on her peanut butter milkshake. Her fourth in two days. Her father leaned down and patted her hand. She wanted to yank it away. She wanted to tell everyone to go away, but didn't have the heart to actually voice the words.

Luke stood on the other side of the hospital room, leaning a shoulder against the wall, his arms crossed over his chest, his narrowed eyes taking in the scene. His face was a mask, betraying nothing of his feelings, but Kate knew him well. He was uncomfortable around her family and her family barely tolerated his presence. Her brothers shot him evil glances when they thought she wasn't looking and if they happened to pass by him, they nudged him a little with their shoulders. He took the ill-treatment without a word.

Her anger grew each minute they were all in the room together. Their behavior toward the man she loved infuriated her. She took another sip of her milkshake, reaching the end with a loud slurp.

"I know you want to go home, honey," her father said, patting her hand yet again. "As soon as the doctor releases you, we'll take you home."

She shook her head and placed her empty cup on the table. "No, daddy. I don't want to go back to your house, that's not home."

Her father paused, shooting her mother a concerned look. Her mother simply shrugged, a small smile on her lips.

"It's not safe for you to go back to your place, Kate. You need someone to take care of you while you recover." He shot Luke a scowl. Her brothers, brainless twits that they were, did the same. Kate barely controlled the urge to roll her eyes. At least Eric wasn't here. As soon as her fever broke and she started feeling better, he'd headed back home.

She shook her head again. "I don't want to go back to my house, either."

She glanced at Luke. He hadn't moved, but his stillness betrayed the fact he was listening. They hadn't had much time together since she'd awoken from her surgery. Part of that was because Luke's boss had monopolized his time, and part of it was because her family hadn't allowed them any time together.

Eric was the one who had told her about Suzanne Carmichael's deception and betrayal of the men who worked under her. That woman had better be glad she was safe and sound in prison because Kate would have had no problem hunting her down and making her pay for what she'd done to Luke and John.

Suzanne Carmichael had ruined so many lives, had taken Luke from her and had permanently scarred a great man like John Callahan. But Suzanne was already getting her just reward. While she languished in jail, Bradley had gone into hiding, hunted by the media he'd courted just days ago. Allegations of price fixing and corruption abounded. His party had dropped him. Suzanne's name was whispered everywhere, everyone stunned that she'd sold American arms to the terrorists they had vowed to fight. She was the epitome of evil to a lot of people.

The Carmichaels had lost their political and social power. For Kate it wasn't enough, but it was a start.

She stared at Luke, willing him to look at her. Her memories of the shooting and the ensuing days were wrapped in a thick fog, but she did remember Luke telling her—not asking—that they were going to get married. And she planned on making him come through with that offer. Soon.

"Kate, honey, if our house isn't your home and your house isn't your home, then where do you want to go?" Her father's voice held trepidation.

She refused to take her eyes off Luke. His gaze bore through her, demanding she answer the question. He was so arrogant. So proud. So hurt. She couldn't imagine what had gone through his mind after discovering Suzanne Carmichael's secret dealings. Her heart ached that she hadn't been there to help him through it.

She shifted her attention to her father's confused expression. "I want to go home, Daddy."

His scowl deepened and she suspected he knew where this was headed and didn't like it one bit. "And where's home, Katherine?"

She smiled, her gaze searching for and finding Luke's.

"Catawba Lake, Tennessee."

A slow smile formed on Luke's mouth, growing in intensity and love. She held out her hand to him. He pushed away from the wall and walked to her, brushing past Riley, then Paul. Barely acknowledging her father when he stepped aside. Luke took her hand in his, and knelt before her.

"You did say you wanted to marry me, didn't you?"

He laughed, the sound rich and vibrant, devoid of ghosts and old pains. "I seem to recall saying something like that. In between demands for milkshakes."

"I'm holding you to it." She squeezed his fingers. Her own fingers had lost the swelling and mobility had returned. The doctors assured her she would be able to draw and paint again.

"Of course you are," he said.

"Thank you for passing out on my doorstep."

He smiled again. "I aim to please."

"Now, take me home."

Luke dropped anchor and headed through the inside of the houseboat to fix Kate an iced tea. His foot hit something and he stumbled. Cursing under his breath, he picked up one red flip-flop. By the time he made it to the kitchen, his arms were full of Kate's drawings, discarded pencils, a potato chip bag and the other missing shoe. He dropped it all in a basket meant for her stuff. He'd tried and failed to bring some semblance of order to Kate's life, but she was such a free spirit, always caught up in the moment, that she inevitably forgot, and he found he didn't really care.

Forgetting about the iced tea, he walked past the bedrooms

and opened the door to the stern. He stopped short, the breath lodged in his throat, still unable to believe she was here, that she was his. And by God, she was *his*. Forever. That had a mighty nice ring to it.

Kate had insisted he bring her to the houseboat, ignoring every objection her father and brothers voiced. Her mother had been silent, eventually shooing the McAuley men out of the hospital room. But that hadn't been the end of Kate McAuley's orders. It'd taken some doing on everyone's part, including Rafferty's. A decoy had to be set up, whisking away an operative who looked like Kate, taking the media off the real Kate's tail. He and Kate snuck out and took the long drive home to Catawba Lake. With a short stop along the way at a justice of the peace.

In the middle of Nowhereville, Tennessee, Kate McAuley, finally, *finally*, became Kate Barone. His wife.

Kate looked up at him, tilting her head against the chaise lounge, her smile bright and happy. Her skin was still pale, too pale for his liking, and he frowned. She frowned back, mimicking him. "Quit worrying. I'm fine."

"You shouldn't have ridden on the back of the three-wheeler." He took the seat next to her, studying her wan pallor.

"How else was I supposed to get home?"

Rembrandt walked up and curled around Luke's ankles. He reached down and plopped the feline in Kate's lap. Picasso was due to arrive in a few weeks, when her family came for a *short* visit.

He leaned over and kissed her nose. "I love you, Kate Barone."

She rubbed her nose against his. "Love you too, Luke Barone." She scooted over and patted the space next to her. Luke fit himself in, draping his arms across her shoulder. She nestled her head on his chest and breathed a deep sigh of contentment.

The sun lowered over the treetops, all bright golds and reds, oranges and yellows. Luke's own sigh of contentment escaped him and he leaned his cheek on the top of Kate's head.

He'd finally found what he'd been searching for the past eighteen months.

Happiness.

Contentment.

Love.

Kate.

About the Author

To learn more about Sharon Cullen, please visit www.sharoncullen.net. Send an email to Sharon at sharoncullen.net or join her Yahoo! group to join in the fun with other readers as well as Sharon! http://groups.yahoo.com/group/Sharon_cullen

Pretending to be newlyweds is a dangerous game...
particularly if you're falling in love.

Holding Her Own
© 2008 Marie-Nicole Ryan

FBI Special Agent in Charge Caitlin Chaney believes in doing things strictly by the book. It's the only way to prove she's earned her rank despite her father's position in the federal government. Just her luck, she's been teamed with an agent who's known for following his instincts, not the rules. To her way of thinking, Agent Jake LeFevre is a screw up and bound to trash her operation—and career.

Jake is used to running undercover ops his way, and he's not too happy with his new boss—an accountant, no less, whose undercover experience is limited at best. He needs a partner who can hold her own, not a prima donna.

At first the sparks that fly between them aren't the good kind. From the very beginning, their cover as madly-in-love newlyweds at a New Orleans casino is tested to the max. But as they work together to find a missing whistleblower in a money-laundering scheme, their admiration grows to respect—and something more.

Then Jake discovers the casino CFO is someone he loved as a teenager. If the woman recognizes him, things could go sideways, and fast—and in a way that could leave their bodies—and hearts—in pieces.

Available now in ebook and print from Samhain Publishing.

Enjoy the following excerpt from Holding Her Own...

Caitlin sat up with a start. She must've fallen asleep after all. The other side of the bed was empty, but the sheets were still warm from his body. Where was he? "Jake? Are you all right?" Of course he was all right. In the air was the smell of fresh coffee brewing.

"Better." He shuffled around in the kitchen, opened a cabinet, then set a couple of cups on the counter. "Mind if I turn on a light?"

"Go ahead." She swung her legs over the side of the bed. Her bare feet on the cold wood floors sent a shiver through her body; she pulled her PJ top tighter. "Coffee smells good."

He avoided her gaze.

She said, "There's no reason to feel awkward about our sleeping together. Nothing really happened."

"Something did happen. The connection between us—it's real, but you're right. Getting involved is a bad idea anytime and with another agent—my boss?

"I don't know if it's right or wrong. I feel too much to hide it anymore." She reached up and caressed his cheek. The stubble against her fingers, the hard plane of his face—when had he grown so dear?

He captured her hand and kissed the tips of her fingers. "Still a bad idea, Kate."

But he didn't let go. Instead, he pulled her closer into a kiss, a long senses-drugging kiss. His lips were hard and demanding. She opened her mouth to him and met his tongue, battling for dominance. The warmth in her belly flamed into a fire. All will, all resistance was for nothing. Her knees weakened. His body was hard against hers.

She'd thought to comfort him, yet his presence and his scent comforted her like nothing she'd ever known. She managed to whisper his name as he picked her up and carried her to the bed.

"Are you sure? Still a bad idea."

"But nothing in life is sure. I just feel..."

"Chèr, you have it right. Feelings are all that matter."

"*Now* is all that matters."

He settled her carefully on the bed, but she pulled him down with her. Poised over her, he unbuttoned her pajamas slowly, prolonging the torture. She wanted him. The backs of his hands grazed her nipples. They tightened into tiny nubs as he slipped her PJ top off her shoulders.

"You're so beautiful. Like I always imagined."

"You imagined me naked?"

"Many times. Dreamed 'bout doing this, too." He bent over and kissed her neck. "Only you didn't talk so much."

"Then shut me up, Jake."

He let out a low growl. His mouth fastened on hers and a thrill ran though her body. He tasted of chicory. His tongue swept against hers. He tugged his shirt free and whipped it over his head while sunlight played over his chiseled muscles. She reached out and caressed the hard muscles of his chest, and it was his turn to shiver.

He kissed her again, this time like a man starving with a deep hunger.

A hunger as fierce as her own.

He slipped a hand between their bodies and touched the damp folds between her legs. Heat blazed again, flushing her body with fire. A whimper forced its way through her lips.

"Did I hurt you?"

"No," she gasped. "I need you. God, I need you so much."

He groaned and buried his face between her breasts. "Soft. So soft." His teeth fastened gently on her nipple and tugged.

Pain, an exquisite pain, morphed into whirlpools of pleasure and swirled from her tightened nipples to her groin. She moaned. He was too slow; she wanted him to fill her...she wanted the heat of his body against hers. Through his jeans, his rigid hard-on pressed against her thigh.

"Take 'em off." She fumbled with the button and zipper of his jeans. Levered on one elbow, he arched away from her slightly and freed his dick. She grasped his firm length; his shaft jerked and pulsed at her touch.

"Easy," he warned. "Or this'll be over too soon."

She managed a gasp. "We wouldn't want that."

"No, we wouldn't." A chuckle rose deep from his chest.

He reached back and shoved his jeans below his knees, then kicked them off.

The heat of his skin against hers sent a thrill though her entire body.

His body. Warm. Hard...and so close.

She pressed upward and gasped his name.

He stilled her with a slow, sensual kiss, then, his breath warm against her ear, he nibbled the lobe. "I've wanted you for so long...from the first moment you walked into Jose's office."

"Hush. Show me." What was it about him that turned her into a pool of need? No man had ever stirred her emotions like Jake.

"Anything for the boss."

"You have to get over that."

"I'm gonna get over *you*, chèr." He nudged her thighs apart and slid two fingers deep into her wet core. "'Bout the time I break the bank at Monte Carlo."

Her inner muscles clenched tight around his fingers as he moved them in and out of her slick folds. He raked the back of her thigh with his thumb.

She bit the inside of her bottom lip as a surge of pleasure ripped though her.

Why this man? Why could he touch her like no man ever had? Not just her body but her heart.

And she could get used to sharing a bed with him.

GET IT NOW

MyBookStoreAndMore.com

GREAT EBOOKS, GREAT DEALS . . . AND MORE!

Don't wait to run to the bookstore down the street, or waste time shopping online at one of the "big boys." Now, all your favorite Samhain authors are all in one place—at MyBookStoreAndMore.com. Stop by today and discover great deals on Samhain—and a whole lot more!

Samhain
publishing ltd

WWW.SAMHAINPUBLISHING.COM

GREAT
CHEAP
FUN

Discover eBooks!

THE FASTEST WAY TO GET THE HOTTEST NAMES

Get your favorite authors on your favorite reader, long before they're out in print! Ebooks from Samhain go wherever you go, and work with whatever you carry—Palm, PDF, Mobi, and more.